The Handle
and the Key

The Handle and the Key

John Neufeld

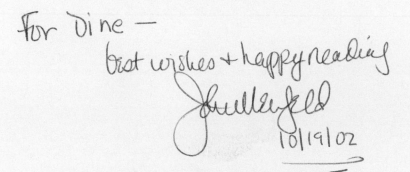

For Dine —
best wishes + happy reading

John Neufeld
10/19/02

Phyllis Fogelman Books
New York

Published by Phyllis Fogelman Books
An imprint of Penguin Putnam Books for Young Readers
345 Hudson Street
New York, New York 10014
Copyright © 2002 by John Neufeld
All rights reserved
Designed by Lily Malcom
Text set in Janson
Printed in the U.S.A. on acid-free paper
1 3 5 7 9 10 8 6 4 2
Library of Congress Cataloging-in-Publication Data
Neufeld, John.
The handle and the key / John Neufeld.
p. cm.
Summary: When Dan, a foster child who has lived in
many homes in his short life, is adopted, he has a hard time
believing that his new family is really permanent.
ISBN 0-8037-2721-6
[1. Foster home care—Fiction.   2. Adoption—Fiction.]   I. Title.
PZ7.N4425 Han 2002
[Fic]—dc21   2001051299

With gratitude to
Kay and Tom Key
Ellie and Tom Colston

The Handle
and the Key

Part I

1

They stood looking at one another, standing close but not touching. Over their heads, strung across the doorway to the dining room, was a banner that read, in multicolored Magic Marker: "Happy Birthday, Dan!"

Mary Kate turned, as directed by her mother, to look directly into the camera. Her brown hair was long and straight, her dark eyes fearless. Dan looked to one side of the lens, his blue eyes focused on the floor near where "Father" stood, as blond as he was.

"Mother" took the picture, hunkering down on her

knees despite the growing bulge of her pregnancy, holding a tiny camera steady, urging both Mary Kate and Dan to smile. Neither did.

As "brother" and "sister," they had met again the night before. Mary Kate had a vague memory, one of many that involved younger children. Dan's senses rang, but only with a sense of place.

"O.K. now, here we go. Just one more to be safe," said "Mother."

Mary Kate stared directly at the lens, scowling. Dan didn't raise his eyes.

The flashbulb blinded Mary Kate, but she stood a moment stonily, waiting for the colored spots to disappear.

Dan was uncertain what to do now that the pictures had been taken. Where was he supposed to go? Was he supposed to speak?

The celebration was a mystery to them both.

"I don't believe you," Mary Kate told her mother in the kitchen as they cut into the birthday cake and put slices on paper plates.

"You don't have to, darling," said her mother. "Your father and I remember, and that should be enough for you."

Mary Kate never whined. She insisted. "I must have been a child," she announced.

Her mother smiled and nodded. "You were. Maybe two years younger than you are now."

"Oh, come on!"

Mrs. Knox nodded her head again. "It's perfectly all right, dear," she said. "Lots of us have trouble with memory as we grow older."

"I certainly don't!" Mary Kate replied forcefully. It was not easy for Mary Kate to admit error. Her brow furrowed. "Well, what do you expect?" she asked suddenly. "You've had more kids in here than Mother Hubbard. Every time I look around, you've got another kid. Floyd, LaKesha, Shirley, Barney, Sam." She paused. "What I don't get is why. Aren't I enough for you?"

"Of course you are, darling," her mother said soothingly. "And you know why we do this."

"We?"

"Your father and I. And you also, really."

"And that good reason would be?"

Her mother smiled and reached out to touch Mary Kate's shoulder. "We have talked about all this before, dear."

"For heaven's sake!" Mary Kate cried. "Just because you talk about something doesn't mean everyone agrees!"

"We don't 'talk' about things, Mary Kate. We share."

"Well, sharing doesn't always mean we're happy."

"No, I know it doesn't," her mother said. "But I've

always thought that talking together, spilling some tension maybe, allows people to see life a little more clearly."

"We live in different worlds," Mary Kate said flatly. Then she picked up two plates and started for the kitchen door. Almost under her breath, she said again, "Every time I turn around, you've got a new kid in here. It's hard to remember them all." She paused and cleared her throat. "One thing, I sure think birthday cake for breakfast can't be healthy. Especially for you!"

Mrs. Knox patted her stomach. "I'll cut back somewhere else," she told her daughter, turning then to open the top of the refrigerator door to reach into its freezer compartment for peppermint-stick ice cream.

Dan saw the small pile of carefully wrapped gifts beside his place at the dining room table. He stood silently near what had been announced as "his" chair the night before. Suddenly, all he wanted to do was run back upstairs into his new room and dive under the covers to hide. What was he doing here? Who were these people? He did have some kind of feeling about the *place*, but he couldn't put any of these people in it.

"Come on, son," said "Father." "Sit down and open one. They're all for you."

Dan looked up at the man beside him. He was tall and thin. He had light curly hair and wide blue eyes. He wore strange glasses that sat on the end of his nose, so that he looked over the top of their lenses at most of the world. Dan was relieved that the man wore suspenders rather than a belt to hold up his striped trousers.

There were too many questions floating in Dan's mind. But there was also, from long habit, something telling him to do as he was told. If he did, there was less likelihood of trouble.

He settled into his chair and looked at the pile of presents, reaching for one without enthusiasm. Usually his hunches were right. That was what was important to remember. Some strange sense of the future could save him.

"Not that one!" Mary Kate said sternly as she put the birthday cake on the table.

Dan looked up quickly.

"No." Mary Kate shook her head. "You should open this one first."

Dan looked where she pointed. It was a larger package than the one he had chosen, and looked heavier.

"Go ahead, son," said "Father."

But "Father" hadn't picked for him. How was he to select? What would happen if he disobeyed his new "sister"?

He tried to look sideways at Mary Kate, but was caught in the attempt. "For heaven's sake," she said impatiently, "what are you waiting for?"

Dan couldn't answer. Who was she? How old was she? She was older than he was, he could figure that out. And taller. Her voice was sharper, too. He closed his eyes for a fraction of a second, hoping to grab hold of some internal warning that would tell him what to do. But none came to him. He was on his own.

The girl was meaner than the man. He reached for the larger present.

2

After breakfast Dan was dressed in brand-new clothes that fit him perfectly. "Mother" drove him and Mary Kate to a school where he was introduced to his teacher, Ms. Breeze. He was left in her room, and then introduced to his new classmates. He was shown his seat and his desk, and given paper, pencils, and books.

The package Mary Kate had insisted he open contained a book bag to be slung over his shoulders and filled with his schoolwork. Also he had been given, before leaving "home," a brand-new lunch box with cartoon characters on its sides and top.

He ate lunch beside his new classmates silently. A couple of girls came over to say hello, but Dan was able only to look up and nod. The girls walked away.

At recess Dan stood on the playground, watching and listening. There was a whirl of running and jumping and shouting all around him. He was a still center, watching, waiting. He scanned the graveled yard, trying to see his "sister," Mary Kate. For a second he thought he had found her, but if it were she, she turned from him quickly and ran farther away with other girl friends.

"You want to play tag?"

Dan was startled. He hadn't seen anyone coming toward him. The boy who now stood at his side wasn't much taller than he was, and he seemed O.K. He wore glasses in clear plastic frames.

"What?" Dan asked.

"Do you want to come and play tag with us? It's fun."

Dan hadn't any idea what the boy was talking about. "No, I don't think so."

"But this is what we do at recess," explained the boy. "We play."

Dan nodded. He thought he understood. "What's your name?" he asked suddenly, surprising himself.

"Brian. Brian Baldwin. Why won't you play tag?"

Dan felt that if he told the truth—that he didn't know

what "tag" was or how to play it—Brian would make fun of him. "I have a cold," he made up quickly.

"Oh," said Brian. "Then you're not supposed to run and get sweaty."

"Right."

"O.K. Maybe tomorrow."

"Maybe."

Dan wondered if he could ask "Mother" or "Father" what this game was and how it was played when he got "home."

At the end of the day Mary Kate arrived outside Dan's classroom. "Mom's outside," she said, turning then to lead Dan out of the school toward a circular driveway.

There were many cars there. Dan couldn't remember what "Mother's" car looked like. He didn't need to. Mary Kate strode decisively toward a deep red van and slid back the rear passenger door for Dan before opening the front passenger door for herself.

"Not again!"

Mary Kate whirled around to face Toby Carter, a boy in her own class. He was thin and well-dressed, and stood putting all his weight on his right leg, his left turned slightly outward.

Dan slipped into the van, and pushed its door closed again, quickly. He didn't like the tone of voice of Mary Kate's friend.

"What do you mean, not again?"

"Another poor, starving urchin saved?"

"He's not poor and he's not starving. And what's it to you, anyway?"

Toby Carter shrugged smugly. "Just need to keep track of the landscape," he explained. "Might be another chapter."

Mary Kate pushed closed the passenger door at her side. She lowered her voice and moved right up to stand chin to chin with Toby Carter. "As a matter of fact," she said in a voice just above a whisper, "this one we're keeping!"

With that, she pulled open the passenger door of the front seat again, got into the car, and slammed the door after her. "What a creep!"

"Who is that, dear?" asked her mother as the van edged into traffic.

"Toby Carter," Mary Kate explained. "He sticks his nose into everything. Everything mean he does, he excuses by saying that he's going to be a writer, a reporter, and if he doesn't ask rude questions or say terrible things, how will he ever find the truth? I hate him!"

"Surely not, Mary Kate," cautioned her mother. "Hate is such a terrible thing."

At home again, Dan was instructed to take off his school clothes and put on clothing in which he could play. He stood in his new room upstairs, looking into a closet in which were hung lots of different and new things. Suddenly he realized that not everything was the same size. There were clothes for kids smaller than he, and some for taller ones, too. Not everything really was new.

What did this mean? Was he just the latest new boy in the house? What had happened to the others?

For a moment Dan shivered. Not knowing things was the worst part of being alive. It meant you could be surprised. It meant things you thought were yours weren't. It meant that what made you happy one day could disappear the next, forever.

He was standing motionlessly in front of the open closet doors when "Mother" entered the room behind him. Despite the fact that she was soon going to have a baby, she was trim and neat, with hair like her daughter's. She had dimples when she smiled, which, to Dan, was reassuring. "It's a lovely fall afternoon, Dan," she said helpfully. "The sun is still up. Why don't you put on your windbreaker?"

Dan nodded. He couldn't imagine at what he was supposed to play, so he didn't have a clue as to what to choose to put on. And he didn't know what a "windbreaker" was.

"Mother" reached into his closet and brought out a deep blue jacket, which she held up for him. "Turn around, Dan, dear," said "Mother." He did. "All right, now give me your right arm."

"Mother" helped him into the jacket. "There! You look just fine. Now, why not go outside and explore?"

Dan nodded and followed "Mother" down the staircase toward the front door. "Have fun, darling," she suggested, holding the door open for him.

Dan stood on the top step outside the house. What was he supposed to do? Play. But at what? With whom? In his last house, he had chores to do, from early morning until day's light disappeared. Or else. No one there had ever suggested he "have fun" and "play."

He walked carefully down the steps and stood on dark green, spiky grass next to the walkway that led up from the street. His arms were at his sides. He heard birds nearby. He turned his head and, without thinking, he began to walk toward their music.

Birds he knew about.

"He just stands there!" Mary Kate announced.

"He's getting his bearings, I imagine," said her mother as she reached into their refrigerator.

"He's totally spaced out!" Mary Kate continued her commentary. "It's like he doesn't even know where he is. Maybe he's a nerd in disguise. A dweeb!"

"Well, darling, what would you do, in a new city, a new house, with people around you don't remember?"

"Ask questions, for one thing!" Mary Kate was definite.

"Dan's shy, Mary Kate," said her mother softly. She smiled. "That's one of the reasons your father and I were so taken with him. He's terribly shy and very polite."

"He just doesn't know anything to say!"

"This is very new to him, dear. After all, if you couldn't remember him from before, how could he remember you?"

"So," Mary Kate demanded, ignoring her mother's comment, "where's he been in the meantime?"

"Since he was here last?"

Mary Kate nodded that that was exactly what she meant. She kept watch, through a kitchen window, on the object of her curiosity.

"We're not all that sure," Mrs. Knox replied. "He was with us for such a short time before the state retrieved him and sent him somewhere else."

"Why'd they do that?"

"Well, I'd guess they thought they had found a good home for him. After all, being a foster child ideally is only temporary."

"And now he's back here with us." Mary Kate looked over her shoulder at her mother. "So, wherever he was, being adopted, I mean, didn't work out. Why, I wonder."

"You don't need to know that, dear."

"Do you?"

"Enough." Mrs. Knox smiled contentedly. "Dan is ours now. We went to a lot of trouble to find him, to get him back. And now he's your brother."

"My *adopted* brother," Mary Kate clarified.

Mrs. Knox cracked two eggs into a ceramic bowl. "Yes, Mary Kate. You may call him that if you want. It's not terribly nice, but it is true."

"Does he know he's been adopted?"

"I'm not sure how much he understands yet, dear. But we're not going to keep any secrets from him. We want him to know who he is and where he came from. That he won't have to leave *this* family. That we love and support him, no matter what."

"No matter what?" Mary Kate seemed astonished. "You mean, he can get away with anything?"

"No," said her mother, "that is not what I mean. He'll learn to live by the same rules you do, and share the tasks we all have."

"How do you know he's not from a family of axe-murderers?"

Mrs. Knox laughed. "What's that supposed to mean?"

"Well, you talk about wanting him to know where he came from and who he is. I bet you don't know very much about that either."

"Your father and I know enough, dear," said her mother evenly.

"And you're not going to tell me?"

"What difference would it make? Dan is here now, and part of our family. He may have had some hard times in the past. We're going to try to erase those events from his memory, with love and attention."

"What hard times?" Mary Kate no longer looked out the window. She was facing her mother.

"I don't think you need to know about that, dear," her mother said firmly.

"So what makes him so special you adopted him?"

Mrs. Knox shook her head. "Mary Kate, this was a little boy, all alone in the world, who had been shifted from one home to another for his whole life. Your father and I felt we had something better to offer." She paused a moment then, smiling to herself. "Besides, he looks a little like your father as a boy."

Mrs. Knox turned away from her daughter then, still smiling for a second before she became more serious. Her voice was very low. "If you want to know, darling, I think we do have a little problem with Dan."

"What's that?" Mary Kate said eagerly.

"Well, there's a lot locked up inside him, Mary Kate. In spite of all the work I've done with children and their families, I'm not sure I can find the key to unlock Dan's heart. And I'm not at all certain even Dan knows where the handle or the key is."

Mary Kate was disappointed in this confidence. "Well, all I can say is that I am certainly surprised."

"By what in particular?" asked her mother, facing her daughter once more. "We've been foster parents before. You've had other 'brothers' and 'sisters' before."

"For your information, Mother, that wasn't so easy, explaining things to everyone and all."

"What things?"

"Who this new kid, or that one, was. Why they were living with us. And then, later, why they didn't live with us."

"I'm sorry you found that so trying," said Mary Kate's mother.

"Well, I did, you know. You forget that kids need to explain their parents' behavior to other kids. As a psychologist, surely you understand that?"

Mrs. Knox smiled. "I do."

"One more thing," Mary Kate pressed. "Since you're going to have another baby of your own, who needs Dan now? I mean, just forget about me for a minute. What about the baby?"

Mrs. Knox stirred the eggs thoughtfully. "I don't think it's a question of who needs Dan, dear. It's more a question of what he needs."

"Sounds to me like you think he's special," Mary Kate decided. She was not pleased.

"Every child I've ever met and worked with is special, Mary Kate." She reached out to pinch her daughter's cheek lightly. "Even you."

Mary Kate drew back and sniffed. "Especially me!"

"You should be inside if you've got a cold."

Dan spun quickly, looking for the voice.

"Over here," Brian Baldwin said, waving a few fingers through a gap in a stockade fence that surrounded Dan's new backyard.

Dan walked to the fence.

"I live right behind you," Brian volunteered.

Dan nodded.

"What are you doing?"

Dan shrugged. "Playing."

"What at?"

"I don't know," Dan admitted. "I like hearing birds. I guess I wanted to see where they were. What kind."

"Are you a bird-watcher?" Brian asked. "There's a special name for that, but I can't remember what it is."

"I don't know it."

"Never mind. Let me ask you a question."

Dan leaned against the fence. "What?"

"Where'd you come from?"

"Where'd *you* come from?" Dan returned.

"I don't mean *that*, babies and all," Brian explained. "I

just meant, well, here you are, part of the Knoxes. There have been a lot of kids in and out of their house, staying for a while."

Dan froze where he stood. He wanted to ask what had happened to the others. He was too afraid. He thought of all the clothing in his closet, the different pants and shirts and jackets of varying sizes. The kids who had worn those—where were they now? Were they even alive?

"Are you their cousin or something?"

Dan tried to think, but his insides were roiling. "Maybe." It was a better answer than what he expected.

"You don't know?"

"I could be," Dan allowed. "A cousin."

"Are you?"

"I've got to go in now," Dan said quickly, already moving away from the fence gap.

Brian's question and his own answer echoed in Dan's mind as he rounded the front of the house.

He knew what he should have answered. He should have said, "No, I'm a foster child."

But that was confusing even to him. If he were a foster child, which, after all, he'd been most of his life, then why suddenly did he have a last name that was new? And if he did have a real new last name, then *who* was he? He wasn't Daniel Johnson any longer. Why was that? How could people change who someone else was so easily? And why would they want to?

He sat on the front steps, looking into the sky, thinking.

Alone, he was calmer. Maybe his new "family" had been foster parents before. Nothing terrible need to have happened to other kids. They just moved on. The same way he had done so often.

But now he had a new name. That had never happened before. What was expected of him? If he had a new identity, maybe he was also expected to behave in a special new way. Who would tell him?

Maybe the Knoxes would have kept the other children, the ones Brian mentioned, if they had been able to figure out what the family's rules and regulations were. What was allowed and what wasn't. How to speak. How to "play."

He would have to try to discover the secret boundaries, the lines over which he could not step if he wanted to stay. Did he? Want to stay?

He closed his eyes against the fading sun.

From his past, images floated behind his eyelids. He tried to push each one away, but another just as bad came in its place. He concentrated on the house behind him. He squeezed his eyes tightly shut and thought about the sensation he'd had on his "birthday."

He did remember something. The house was sort of

comfortable to him. The people weren't. There had been so many in such a short span of years. He thought he remembered "Father's" suspenders, and the feeling of relief he might have had before when he saw them.

The sound of a car engine made him open his eyes to see "Father's" car coming up the gravel driveway. It passed him on the steps. "Father" waved at him before disappearing into a garage that had been opened . . . by magic!

3

"Mother" came into his bedroom just as she had done the night before.

"Sleepy?"

Dan nodded.

Mrs. Knox walked around Dan's bed, tucking in stray covers. Then she sat halfway down its length and reached out a hand toward Dan's. She took it. "Teeth brushed?"

Dan nodded again.

"Feeling a little confused?" Mrs. Knox asked quietly,

squeezing Dan's hand lightly. He did not return the pressure.

"I don't know."

Mrs. Knox smiled. "Well, I think I do, dear. Here you are, new people, new school, new house. You must have a thousand questions. I certainly would have."

Dan thought about asking how one played tag but said nothing.

"Mother" sat without moving for a moment, not speaking, waiting. "Well, Dan dear, there's one answer I want to give you even if you haven't asked the question."

Dan waited.

"You're here for keeps. We love you. We're thrilled you're in our home."

"Mary Kate, too?" Dan asked.

Mrs. Knox smiled. "Of course, dear. Mary Kate as well. Sometimes she doesn't show things as easily as your father and I do. But she does have feelings, Dan, good ones. Maybe by the time you begin to feel a little more at ease, she will, too."

Dan was unconvinced.

"You can help us all, dear, you know," Mrs. Knox added then.

Dan couldn't think how.

"We know, your father and I, some bits and pieces about your life before you arrived here. I'm sure you had many happy moments. But you may also have had some bad ones."

Dan waited.

"If there are things"—Mrs. Knox picked her way slowly and carefully toward her goal—"that we three do, things that might upset you . . . especially because they seem so much like other things that have happened to you in the past . . . well, I guess what I'm asking from you, Dan, is that you tell us what they are. We're bound to say the wrong thing, sometimes. Or do the wrong thing. Things that will bring back bad memories."

Mrs. Knox squeezed Dan's hand tightly. "You can help us be the family you want us to be, dear, is what I'm trying to say. Do you understand?"

Dan nodded.

"Sleep tight, darling," "Mother" said then, standing and then leaning down to kiss his forehead.

Dan closed his eyes.

When he heard the door to his room closing, Dan rolled over and burrowed his head under his pillow. He'd wait and see. What "Mother" said sounded nice, but other people in his life had said pretty much the same things.

And he had been returned anyway.

Worse, in the past when he had said something about what had happened to him before, other families thought he was complaining. And when someone in authority thought you were complaining, he or she usually made certain you had something more to complain of the next day.

He remembered people telling him, "If you think that's bad, kiddo, wait." And when he had been even smaller than he was now, if he cried, more often than not he heard, "What are you crying for? You want something to cry about? I'll give you something to cry about!"

Dan wasn't going to cry. He wasn't going to complain. He wasn't going to talk about things that upset him.

That much about life he understood.

4

Just as "Mother" was backing her van out of the garage in order to take Mary Kate and Dan to school again, another car stopped in front of the house. Its ignition was turned off. A woman, older than "Mother," got out and waved to Mrs. Knox.

"Back in fifteen minutes!" shouted Mrs. Knox to this woman, who nodded and walked up toward the front door of the Knoxes' house.

"That's Mrs. Farrow," "Mother" explained, turning halfway around in her seat to look at Dan. "She comes in every week to help with some of the household cleaning. You'll like her, Dan."

Dan nodded. He didn't know what else was expected of him.

In class Dan sat quietly, looking as though he understood what was being said and trying to follow directions. But often, when he wasn't nervously obeying Ms. Breeze, his mind wandered.

He'd been in a school once before, although not for very long. Long enough to begin to sense what the rules *there* were, and how to behave. And he did understand why he was in school. He was there to learn.

But learning wasn't always easy. His mind was too crowded with images and memories of before, of people and events and instructions he had tried so hard to follow. In any quiet moment it was easy to slip back into his memory and to replay what he recalled of earlier times, even though he had been trying forcefully to forget them.

Dan was glad his new teacher, Ms. Breeze, didn't seem to notice these struggles.

What he was thinking about now was Mrs. Farrow. He opened his notebook and thought about starting a list. It was easier to put down pictures than words: a bucket and brush, a log, a ladder. He looked at the page and then added something else. Then he leaned his chin on his hand and thought about the pictures on his list again, hard.

Once, in his own world, Dan even smiled to himself, and nodded positively, adding another sketch.

Ms. Breeze noticed.

5

Dan came tiptoeing down the stairway. He had changed into "play" clothes, but play was the last thing on his mind. He walked toward the kitchen at the back of the house, passing "Mother's" study, in which she read and worked, often alone but sometimes with other people, behind closed doors. Dan had already heard soft voices in the den. He knew enough not to linger to hear, or even to look as though he were.

When he got to the threshold of the kitchen, he stood looking in. Mrs. Farrow was leaning over the sink, scouring it, her back to him. She was stouter than his "mother," with broader shoulders and broader hips. Her hair was two colors: white and yellowish white.

"Hello," Dan said quietly.

Not quietly enough, for Mrs. Farrow spun around as though terrified. "Goodness! You scared the daylights out of me. I didn't hear you coming."

Dan nodded. "I can help you."

Mrs. Farrow smiled nicely. "You'd have to stand on a ladder, my friend, to get up here."

"I can wash the floors," Dan suggested. "If there's a brush and a pail, I can wash the floors."

"Well, now," Mrs. Farrow said as she crossed her arms in front of her chest, "that's the nicest offer anyone's made all day. Trouble is, Daniel, I've already washed the floor. And waxed it."

"I can help with the pans, then," Dan offered, taking a step into the kitchen.

"You're sweet," Mrs. Farrow said. "Tell you what. Why don't I make you a snack?"

Dan looked blank.

"A sandwich, or some cookies. I have time before I leave."

"Oh no," Dan said quickly. "I'm fine. I'm not allowed to eat between meals."

"Who says?"

Dan opened his mouth to speak, but he couldn't

remember a name. He changed course quickly. "In winter I can help you with the logs, the firewood. I'm good at breaking wood up, and sawing."

"Someone your size?" Mrs. Farrow smiled again, surprised.

Dan nodded positively. "And I can help you carry water, too."

Mrs. Farrow nodded and came toward Dan to ruffle the hair at the top of his head. "You're a very talented young man, and I won't forget you offered."

"Really. I can do all those things and more, too."

Mrs. Farrow grinned. "I'll call on you, I promise. In the winter."

Dan stood a moment, not quite satisfied. After a few seconds, when Mrs. Farrow didn't say anything more, he turned and walked back out of the kitchen.

He passed "Mother's" office again and quietly went back upstairs. He stood outside Mary Kate's door. He knocked.

"Yes?"

Dan took a breath before he turned the knob and pushed the door open. Sometimes Mary Kate seemed to be interested in him, sometimes not. He couldn't figure her out.

Mary Kate, her back to the door, was seated at her desk and working at her computer, diligently tackling her homework assignments.

Dan waited a moment, and then cleared his throat.

"What is it?" Mary Kate asked sharply without taking her eyes from the console screen.

Dan inhaled. "I can do washing," he said hesitantly. "I'm not so good ironing, but I'm good at washing and rinsing and hanging out."

Mary Kate hardly seemed to hear. "That's nice."

"I can polish stuff and dust and vacuum or sweep," Dan offered. "I can do almost anything you need."

"O.K.," Mary Kate said distantly. "I'll keep all that in mind."

Dan didn't know what else to say. He stood a moment more, but Mary Kate never turned around. After another moment Dan left the room, noiselessly closing the door behind him.

He walked downstairs and opened the front door.

He sat down on the steps outside and watched cars pass by.

6

"Are you sure we can?" Mary Kate asked at dinner that night. "How can we just go? Will school let us off?"

"They will, for a week or so," said her father, seated at the head of the dining room table, adding cream to his coffee.

Dan looked from one speaker to the other.

"We thought this would give us all a chance to get to know one another better, in a shorter time," said her father, expanding his answer to Mary Kate's questions.

"Besides, if we wait too long to go to the cottage, I'll be

too big to be any help." Mrs. Knox smiled and patted her stomach. "And I wouldn't be able to hike or fish or do anything that's fun."

Dan had never been hiking or fishing. And where was this all supposed to happen?

"We'll leave this Friday morning," said Mr. Knox. "Get a jump on the weekend traffic. We can be there, fire all lit and furniture dusted off by the end of the day."

"You'll like the lake, Dan," said "Mother." "The water's clear and cool and full of fish. We even have a little dock with a rowboat tied up to it."

"Or at least we did when we were last up there. We've had a couple of very big storms since then," added "Father."

Mary Kate and Mrs. Knox stood up from their places and began to clear the table. Dan was left with "Father."

"So, Scout, how was school?"

Scout? Was that his new name?

"It's hard going into a new class, meeting people for the first time. At least I always thought so. How about you?"

"It was O.K.," Dan allowed quietly.

"And how is your teacher?"

Dan shrugged. "Nice, I guess." He remembered suddenly. "Could you tell me what playing tag means, please?"

"Father" put down his coffee cup and leaned toward him. "Is that what you did?"

Dan shook his head.

"Because you didn't know how?"

Dan nodded.

"It's simple, Dan, and fun. A gang of kids gets together and decides who is 'it.' That person has to try to catch someone else, and touch him, in order to make the new person 'it.' Understand?"

"Where is the lake?" Dan asked, only half understanding what "Father" had told him about playing tag.

"About two hundred miles from here. Up north, toward Canada. Or at least, in that direction. We're a long way from Canada."

Canada? Dan lowered his eyes and thought a moment. It was another country, he thought. Somewhere far away. Is that where they were going to take him to leave him?

"Please," said Dan then, an urgency in his voice, "could you tell me what I am supposed to do here?"

"Father's" forehead furrowed. "What do you mean, Dan?"

"Well," Dan said slowly, more afraid of the answers than the question, "I'm new here, you see."

"Father" nodded, waiting.

"I don't know," Dan began, his eyes beginning to fill, "what I am supposed to do. To help or work or anything. Could you tell me, please?"

"Father" stood up from his chair and came behind

Dan's. He put his big hands on Dan's tiny shoulders. "Are you afraid, Dan?"

Dan nodded, his head low.

"Oh, Scout, don't be!" said "Father" then. "You're here because we want you to be safe and to grow up having fun. You don't have to *do* anything to please us. Just give us all, and yourself, too, time to relax, to get to know one another. Don't be afraid. You're here to stay, I promise you."

Dan nodded that he understood. But he wasn't convinced. There were rules and chores and punishment everywhere.

He knew.

7

The Thursday before the Knoxes were to leave for their campsite, Dan followed Mary Kate down a school hallway toward the front doors where "Mother's" van waited once more.

Toby Carter blocked their progress. "So," he said, crossing his arms in front of his chest, "how much do you actually make on each kid?"

"What?" Mary Kate demanded. "What are you talking about?"

"I'm talking about being paid by the state for what you do. Take in kids, I mean."

"You're crazy."

"Not at all," Toby said confidently.

Dan stood at Mary Kate's side, listening.

"We don't need money," Mary Kate announced.

"Well, you get it anyway," Toby informed her. "You get a monthly check from somebody at the capital for taking a kid off the state's hands. I know. I read about it."

"So you think—"

"I don't think, I *know*," Toby broke in. "You've had a whole flock of kids since I've known you, coming and going. You've probably made a lot of money off this."

Mary Kate had forgotten Dan was at her side. "Look, wise guy, my mother is a psychologist and she has always worked with kids. My dad has a terrific job. They figure, and so do I, we can help kids in trouble. There's nothing wrong with that that I can see. You'd probably be a better person if someone took you in! At least it would get you out of my face!"

Toby smiled smugly. "I need to know about this. I may be a mayor when I grow up. So all I wondered was, how much do you get and for how long? It's just a matter of figuring out my budget platform."

"You are such a creep!" Mary Kate almost yelled. "You really are!"

She turned quickly away from Toby Carter and in doing so, saw Dan. She grabbed his hand and pulled him along after her.

"What did you do with it?" demanded Mary Kate.

"Wait a minute, dear," replied her mother. "I'm not at all sure this is the kind of tone I want to hear."

"I'm not interested in tone, Mother. I'm interested in money. I never knew!"

Mrs. Knox nodded agreement. "Nor should you have."

"You don't think I'm old enough to understand you make money off all these kids you take in?"

"I think you're old enough, Mary Kate. I don't think you're wise enough."

"Oh, terrific!" snorted Mary Kate, spinning in frustration. "So, what happened to the wonderfulness of helping poor kids who needed a home? Where'd that go all of a sudden?"

"That, Mary Kate, is the way your father and I feel. That, young lady, is why we opened our home to so many children who needed shelter and affection."

"But you made money off it!"

"Yes, we did," her mother agreed after a moment's pause. "We're not angels, Mary Kate. The state offers aid to families like ours who take in foster children."

"Did you really need it?" demanded her daughter.

"No, probably not. Certainly not after a time. But payment is part of how the state operates its foster child program. It was just part of our bargain."

"God!" Mary Kate sighed angrily. "I am so shocked! So disappointed!"

"Don't be," answered her mother. "The money that concerns you so we spent on you, or at least a good portion of it."

"This gets worse and worse!" shouted Mary Kate at the ceiling of the study.

Mrs. Knox smiled. "No, it doesn't. I went back to school, you know, to get my degree. Your father was working very hard. The money did come in handy. It allowed us to find Mrs. Farrow. To have her here every day to look after you. And as you grew and needed her less, that money went in other directions."

"Such as?"

"Really, Mary Kate, this isn't your concern."

"Really, Mother," Mary Kate mimicked, "it is."

Mrs. Knox stood up from her desk, frowning. Mary Kate took a step back.

"I'm sorry all of this came as a shock to you, Mary Kate. For your information, the money offered families like ours by the state isn't all that enormous. Secondly, it is designed to help us support, clothe, and feed our new little friends. Thirdly, whether or not your father and I used the money for that or another purpose isn't a concern of the state, nor of anyone else. We spent it wisely and well."

Mrs. Knox paused. "Really, I don't think I need to justify this to you, Mary Kate. No child who lived here could have gotten better care or more affection. And none got what we want to give Dan, without, I might add, being paid by anyone."

She turned her back on her daughter and sat again at her desk. After a second she swiveled in her chair. "You know, dear, parents aren't perfect. Sometimes what we do doesn't make sense to our children. Certainly not at first, anyway. But we make decisions based on our sense of what's needed and right. I think you just have to learn to trust us."

"I did! I did trust you!" Mary Kate objected.

"Mary Kate, I am speaking to you as I would to an adult. Believe me. I'm sorry you were shocked and surprised. I am not sorry about what your father and I have done all these years. And now, as your own friends would say, 'get over it.'"

Mary Kate's eyes opened hugely and her mouth grew in proportion. Suddenly, she shut them all before turning and stomping out of the room.

8

Dan had trouble sleeping that night.

There was so much to plan for and so little he actually knew about what he was facing.

It was clear that he was going back.

No one ever drove him anywhere on a long trip that he hadn't ended up being returned to the state.

He didn't have much to pack for the next morning. Usually what had been given to him was taken back. Clothes, toys, books. None of these things ever went with him on his return trips.

What kept him awake that night was trying to figure out, despite what "Father" had said to him at dinner before, where he had failed. He *knew* there were things he should have done or said. There wasn't a house in the world, he thought, that didn't have its rules. Or that didn't have things he was supposed to do when he got into them. Every place he had been was different from this one, but experience taught him he had to learn skills fast, had to get used to doing things in different ways.

He liked "Mother" and "Father." About Mary Kate he wasn't sure. She didn't seem to like him, so he couldn't think why he had to like her. Although he knew deep down that he had to pretend he did. That was one of the rules that always applied. You had to behave as though you liked the people who took you in. You had to be grateful.

And he thought he might be, if only he ever stayed in one place long enough to learn what to be grateful for.

To be away from the state was one thing. If he didn't feel it, others did, other kids, and they had told him.

But they had told him this only when they were returned to the state. After.

They had spun tales of events and treats he couldn't believe to be true. He *wanted* them to be true, but how could he really believe them when what he was told came from kids who clearly hadn't learned the same lesson he had: there are always rules.

He tossed and rolled over in his small bed. Moonlight came through the curtained windows and crossed his bed in streaks.

He had tried. He always did. This time he had even done something he hadn't done before: he had actually asked what the rules were rather than trying to figure them out for himself. Of course, usually people told you right away what was expected, and then it was up to you to do your best to satisfy them.

But if the people here weren't going to help that way, what choice had he but to fail?

It *wasn't* his fault!

He rolled over again and brought his knees up to his chest.

It was. He just wasn't smart enough to understand.

9

The Knoxes were on the road by ten the next morning, heading out of the city toward the north. Traffic was light. Morning rush hour was over.

"Father" drove the van. Behind where Dan sat looking out the window were bedding and foodstuffs and tools and clothing.

Mary Kate sat beside Dan, pointing out landmarks she recognized from earlier trips. Dan was dutiful to look where Mary Kate wanted, and in his mind tried to sound out the signposts they passed. He saw "E-van-ston" pass and "Col-fax" and "Spring-field." He tried to memorize not just the names, but the order in which he passed through these small towns. And then, in his mind, he ran them backward: Springfield, Colfax, Evanston.

The van rose from flatlands into a series of foothills on which were pine trees and streams running down toward some distant sea. Some of the leaves on the trees had already begun to change color. Despite his concern, Dan liked to be driven across bridges, to hear the sounds the van wheels made on different surfaces.

And then, suddenly, something made him sit up straight. Wait a minute, he thought. He hadn't come this way from the state!

This was new territory!

He looked around, to the right and the left and behind the van, his eyes wide and his brain on alert. Think! he told himself. Think back!

It *was* new.

He wanted to say something, to ask.

He didn't want to be told what he thought was wrong.

He sat straight all the way north, looking through the front windshield. Not one town's name was familiar.

He was barely able to keep a smile from his face.

The cabin was made of logs. It had two stories, and a porch that wrapped around three sides of the building, giving out onto a patch of grass that ran down to the lakeside where, just as "Father" had said, there was a dock.

"Father" stopped the van behind the cabin and stepped down onto the ground. He stood a moment, inhaling the clear, crisp air.

"Mother" turned in her seat to look at Dan. "Well, here we are. What do you think?"

Dan was uncertain what to say. "It's nice," he decided.

"Come on, dear, Mary Kate and I will show you around."

"Mother" got out of the van, as did Mary Kate and Dan. "Father" began to unload the back of the car, putting parcels and bundles on the grass in neat order. While Dan was being given his tour, "Father" would bring into the cabin what was needed.

Inside, the house was nicer than Dan had imagined. It had a lot of rooms. It was bigger than it looked. And upstairs were three bedrooms—one for him, one for Mary Kate, and one for "Mother" and "Father."

As Mrs. Knox led Dan and Mary Kate through the cabin, she dusted and cleared and neatened it as she walked.

Mary Kate got off the tour when her own room had been shown. "You know," she said to her mother, "I think I always sleep better up here."

"We all do," said Mrs. Knox. "Come on, Dan, let's look at your room."

"Dan's room" was in the front of the building, over-looking the lake below. There were two pine trees growing closely together by the side of his window. If he opened the window, he could reach out to touch them—if only there weren't screens on the windows.

There was a small closet—a wooden pocket really, covered by a cloth on a rod that was pushed to one side or the other. There was a small wooden bureau, a table near the head of the bed with a lamp on it, and wooden shelves along one wall. What interested Dan most, how-ever, was that the walls inside this log cabin were shiny and smooth, obviously made of the same wood as outside but somehow different, more homey. There was a calen-dar pinned up on one of these, near the small bureau. Its scenes were much like the very view Dan could see through his window.

"Do you think this will do?" asked "Mother."

Dan smiled.

"Good. It's yours, just like at home. Only those people you want to come in can. That's one of our rules."

A rule! Finally!

In just a few days Dan learned how to fish, how to row a boat, how to make a fire in the fireplace and one outside, too, on the ground, in a pit. He also learned how to make certain that such a fire was truly out, forest fires always being a danger.

He learned how to cook on an open fire. He learned how to "police" the area where he was, picking up trash and leftovers to keep the scene clean and clear. He learned how to whitewash stones to be placed along paths, although he already knew how to paint a little.

He learned how to fill and clean birdhouses that dotted the property and hung near the lake's edge. He learned how to tie a few simple knots, especially to keep the little rowboat from leaving the dock and escaping onto the lake all by itself.

He learned what "flapjacks" were.

He learned how to clean dishes at the lakeside.

The Knoxes learned that Dan was good with an axe, that he could whittle, that despite his size he was strong. They learned that anything they asked, Dan was willing to do. He said no to nothing. They learned he had a tiny sense of humor that would surface at odd moments when no one expected it.

In the rowboat, fishing with "Father," Dan couldn't help but be puzzled when his "father" reeled in a fairly big bass and tried to take the hook from its mouth. The fish was slippery and wet, and getting a firm enough grip on it to keep it still and extract the barb wasn't easy. Mr. Knox squirmed and muttered under his breath, and finally, in frustration, said, "Come on, you little bastard, give it up!"

"How do you know," said Dan from the back of the boat as he watched, "that the fish is a bastard?"

Mr. Knox looked up, the fish still wriggling in his hands. "Well, Dan, because I don't imagine his parents were ever married."

"Maybe they were."

"You think so?"

"Sure. In Fishland, maybe they even had a big family."

Mr. Knox chuckled and, after getting the barb out of the bass's mouth at last, threw the fish back into the lake.

"Why'd you do that?" asked Dan. "If you catch him, aren't you going to keep him? Maybe eat him?"

"Next summer," Mr. Knox replied. "When he's even bigger."

"He'll still be a bastard."

Mr. Knox laughed. "He sure will."

Dan took walks with "Mother," exploring the hillsides and cliffs around the lake, learning the names of a few trees and some of the wild berries that were beginning to appear on bushes beside footpaths. He was quick to be able to recognize poison ivy and sumac. He learned how to skip stones across the water.

On rainy mornings he sat quietly as "Mother" read to him, stories about magicians and brave children and horses who ran so hard their hearts burst. She pointed to the pictures on the pages she turned slowly, and to simple words she wanted Dan to remember. Dutifully, he repeated them to her.

And, finally, he learned how to play tag. At first he took the rules of the game very seriously, chasing and hiding with no smile, no sense of pleasure. But then, once he felt secure about what he was doing, for the first time the Knoxes heard Dan's laughter, an excited giggle as he ran and dodged and tried to hide from whoever was "it."

Mary Kate had been absent from a lot of these activities, although she had been persuaded to play tag on the front lawn. "I just can't run the way you do, dear," her mother had said. "I'm carrying too much weight."

"Well, for a while," Mary Kate allowed, putting down a book she had been reading and looking back at the boys pictured on posters all around her room.

"What are you doing, really, dear?" asked her mother.

"What do you mean? When?"

"In terms of Dan," her mother explained. "You seem, well, distant."

Mary Kate shrugged.

"You're not jealous, are you, Mary Kate? That would be so wasteful of all your energy and talent."

"No, not exactly," Mary Kate answered. "I don't know. I'm doing the best I can. After all, he is new and he's not ours, not really. I just don't know what I think."

Her mother smiled and put her arm around her daughter, bringing her into her side and squeezing her. "I hope you'll let me know what you decide. And when."

"Oh, Mom!" Mary Kate groaned, breaking away. "Let's just play tag."

The weekend passed so quickly that "Father" decided they might as well stay a few more days.

Then, before Dan was aware of what was going on, Mr. and Mrs. Knox and Mary Kate were packing up again. The plan was to drive back down to their town in the morning, against traffic getting away from it on the next weekend.

And, Dan knew instantly, they were going to desert him, leave him at the lake, drive away and never return.

As dishes were being put away the night before their departure, Mr. Knox carried a load of them into the kitchen and asked his wife, "Why don't we take a different route down?"

Mrs. Knox turned from the sink and looked at her husband, waiting.

"We could show Dan the state capitol if we took Route Forty-four."

Dan froze at his place, standing there with his hands full of plates and silverware. He could see the Knoxes through the archway of the kitchen and he prayed silently. This was worse than being left behind!

"I don't see why not, dear," said Mrs. Knox then.

"Unless you're not up to the longer ride," Mr. Knox added.

Mrs. Knox smiled. "You'll probably just have to make a few more stops at gas stations for me." She put her hands on the surface of her stomach. "We have an impatient little thing here."

"You're sure it's O.K.?"

"I'll be fine. And I think Dan will be pleased, too."

Dan lay awake.

There was no doubt.

After all, the state paid these people to keep him.

When they grew tired of him, he would be "cashed in."

Despite the fun *he* had had at the lake, the Knoxes *were* like the other families with whom he'd lived. "Father" and "Mother" were nicer than the others, but Mary Kate was just the same. She ignored him as much as she could. She didn't want to be responsible for him. She probably didn't even like having him around.

He had heard other people make up stories, promise treats.

Dan sat up in bed. His stay with the Knoxes had been a vacation, really. *Really*.

But it was over.

10

"He's not up here!" Mary Kate shouted down the staircase the next morning.

"Where could he be?" asked Mrs. Knox. "He has to have breakfast before we go. He'll be starving on the road."

"I'll look outside," Mr. Knox volunteered. "Maybe he's down at the water."

But after ten minutes of looking around and calling for his son, Mr. Knox returned to the cabin, clearly upset. "He's disappeared!"

"He couldn't have. He's much too young to do anything like that."

"Maybe he doesn't want to go home," Mary Kate offered. "Back to school or something."

"We have to find him," Mr. Knox said.

"We will, dear," said his wife, moving a frying pan to a cold burner. "Come on."

All three Knoxes first went upstairs and searched the bedrooms, the closets, the bathroom. Then they descended and went through the living room and the kitchen. Finally they left the house together and, each in a different direction, went into the woods that bordered their property, shouting, "Dan! Dan, where are you? Dan!"

He watched from a crossbar in the branches, balanced safely. The climb up the tree had not been as difficult as he had thought, but he had not dared to look down as he scaled the pine. He was only sorry he hadn't waited until after breakfast to disappear. He could still smell what had been put on hold in the kitchen while they looked for him.

Dan saw Mary Kate and "Father" and "Mother" rush out of the cottage. He had heard them calling his name behind him, indoors. In a way, to hear their shouts had made him happy.

As "Father" disappeared into the woods on one side of the house and "Mother" went to scour the beachfront,

Mary Kate had started to climb the hill behind the house. Apart from the cries of each "Dan! Dan! Where are you?" the air was quiet and windless.

He shifted on his perch to look behind him at the house. He would be able to get into the house by breaking through a screen and climbing into his own room. The distance between where he was now and the screened windows seemed greater than he remembered.

Worse, while he had been almost pushed up the tree by his eagerness to get away to hide, now that he looked back down at the ground, he realized how high he was and how far apart the branches were that he'd used as his stepladder. Getting in, or down, wasn't going to be as easy as he had thought.

"Mother's" van sat loaded and ready at the end of the path down from the main road.

He would miss her.

He would miss "Father," too.

What else could he do? They were going to take him back. They were going to drive him straight to the capital city and cash him in. He would have to put a good face on, tell people there how great things had been. And then he would have to explain why he had been brought back. Once more.

It was too much. He couldn't do it. Better to be on his own, no matter what happened to him.

*   *   *

"Well," said Mr. Knox loudly, standing beside the van, his hand on its top, "we'll just have to go on."

"But George, we can't just lea—"

Mr. Knox's eyebrows rose slightly and he widened his eyes in a signal. "We can't stay here, dear," he explained. "If Dan doesn't want to live with us, there's nothing we can do."

"But he'll be all alone out here," Mary Kate objected. "He's too small to survive." Then the words her father had spoken seconds before snapped into her brain. "Daddy's right, you know. Maybe Dan doesn't want to be here with us. Maybe he hasn't wanted to be anywhere he was."

Mary Kate looked expectantly, first at her mother and then at her father. Neither seemed to have heard.

Mr. Knox walked slowly around to the far side of the van, with his hands waving sideways at waist level.

"But breakfast . . . ?" said his wife.

Mr. Knox pursed his lips.

"I don't get it," Mary Kate said. "What's going on?"

Mr. Knox bent down as though to tie his shoe. "We'll just get in the car, making a lot of noise about leaving. We'll take the van up to the top of the drive and get it on the road. Then you two wait. Dan and I'll be up pretty soon."

"You know where he is?" Mary Kate asked.

Mr. Knox nodded and turned his chin to direct attention back at the house.

"I don't see anything," said his wife.

"In the pine tree, on the right," said her husband. He smiled. "How many pine trees have birds in blue windbreakers sitting in them?"

Mrs. Knox squinted. "I see him," Mary Kate whispered.

"He'll think we're abandoning him," Mrs. Knox said.

"He does already," said her husband.

The three stood a moment, silently, Mr. Knox once again putting his hand on the top of the van. "Let's get ready," he suggested. "Just go about doing what we usually do and then get in the car. I'll drive, but I'll slip out after we hit the road."

As the van was driven slowly up the hill toward the main road, Dan let out a chestful of air.

In a way, he was pleased to be alone. In another way, he was angry. They hadn't really spent a lot of time looking for him. If they'd really cared, they would have done something, even called the police. But that idea was frightening. Who knew? If the police came, maybe he really would be taken away from the Knoxes and cashed in. Maybe the police wouldn't give the Knoxes any choice.

His plan called for an hour's wait before trying either to get into the house from above, or to shinny down the tree trunk and break in some other way. But how long was an hour? And then, when he was inside, what was he going to do?

He didn't imagine he could live there in the cabin forever without being discovered. And no matter how much the Knoxes said they liked him, they couldn't be happy to find him there if and when they came back. By that time, they would have learned to live without him, and he certainly would be taken back to the capital.

Well, when he got inside, he would pack some food. There was stuff in the refrigerator he thought he could use. He didn't imagine he needed much. He wasn't going to hike clear across the country. All he was going to do was walk until he found a house or a farm and then offer to work there. Down deep he felt more comfortable being in the country than the city. And the idea that maybe, for the first time, he could choose his own family—won with hard work and following every rule—excited him.

Time seemed to pass slowly. Dan had no watch. As the minutes passed, he became sad. He wouldn't cry. He was only doing what he had to. To freshen his sense of determination, he tried to get angry . . . at being left again, at being turned back in, at failing—although this time he had really tried. Of course, he reminded himself, he had always tried, but this time he had actually asked people what they wanted of him. It wasn't his fault if the answers weren't clear.

He needed to go to the bathroom.

"Hey, Scout, what's so exciting up here?"

Despite the familiar voice, Dan nearly fell from his branch.

In a funny way, Dan felt relieved.

"Well?" said "Father." "What's the plan?"

Dan shrugged, hugging the center stem of the pine tree.

"Let's try it another way, Dan. Why would you want to stay here alone?" Mr. Knox was leaning against the sash at Dan's front window, talking through it as he began to unscrew its fittings with a pocketknife.

Dan couldn't think what to say. Then he did. "I was going to be alone, anyway."

"You were?" said "Father." "That's news to me."

"You were going to take me back!"

"Who said so?"

"I heard you last night. We were going to the capital."

Mr. Knox stopped what he was doing for a moment. "Do you want to go back?"

"No."

"Well, then, since now we've talked about it like grown-ups, let's forget all that."

"You mean it?"

As Mr. Knox pulled the screen inward and pushed the window sash farther up its track, he cleared his throat. "Dan, some people keep their promises."

Dan waited, still gripping tightly.

"We will, Dan. I promise you."

Dan wanted to believe this.

"Now, how about coming in from there, so we can all drive home?"

Dan looked across the few feet that separated him from "Father."

"Would you rather climb down by yourself?"

Dan looked down at the ground. The height seemed huge. He shook his head.

"Well, then, just lean out toward me. I'll lean out toward you."

"I can't," Dan said with a quaver in his voice.

"You can. I know you can. Come on, son, it's not so far."

Dan waited a minute, trying to make up his mind. Then, without thinking any more about it, he inched out on his branch.

At the same time, Mr. Knox leaned out of the second-story window toward Dan. He stretched out an arm, but found there were still half a dozen feet between them. "Come on, Scout. Just a little more."

Dan sidled carefully on his branch, and came a little closer to the house. Mr. Knox stretched out farther, too.

They both looked at the distance between them. Mr. Knox pulled back into Dan's bedroom and disappeared from view as he slid Dan's bed over to the open window. He hooked his legs under the bed frame and then once more leaned out the window, coming closer now to where Dan sat. "Well, that's some progress, anyway."

Not as far as Dan could tell.

"O.K., Dan, let's switch to plan B, shall we?"

"What's that?"

"You come as far out on your limb as you can, and then, since you're just a little higher than I am, throw yourself toward me. I'll catch you."

"Can you do that, really?"

"Sure I can. We both can. Come on, now. Slide out on the limb till it starts to shake, and then let yourself go."

Dan moved an inch more.

"Come on, son, you can do it."

Dan moved another few inches. "I can't," he said sadly.

"Dan, do you trust me?"

Dan wanted to trust "Father," he really did.

"Just do as I say. Let yourself go. Swing a little toward me and let go."

Dan closed his eyes for a second. When he opened them again, he saw "Father" with his strong arms reaching out for him. He held his breath and inched a little more out on the pine bough. He had made up his mind. He would do it.

But really, deep down, he *couldn't* trust "Father."

"Hang on, Dan!" Mr. Knox shouted. "Hang on tight!"

Their hands had almost touched before Dan sank below "Father's" reach. Without really meaning to, Dan had grabbed a lower branch as he sank so swiftly toward the ground. Now he was hanging there, his other hand wrapped around the limb as well, swinging between the tree and the side of the cabin.

"Stay there, Dan!" "Father" instructed. "Don't move!"

Dan hung silently. He looked down at the ground. It seemed a long way down, and there was a circle of rocks around the base of the tree.

Within seconds "Father" was below him. "Dan? How're you doing?"

Dan nodded he was safe for the moment.

"Father" put a foot on the bottom limb of the tree closest to the house and started up toward its top. The branches beneath his feet began to bend. The tree was tall, but not old or strong.

"Dan, we have a little problem here."

Dan waited.

"See the branch below you, son?" asked "Father."

Dan dared again to look down. "Yes."

"Dan, pretend you're in the circus."

"What do you mean?"

"Haven't you ever seen men on trapezes swinging through the air, hanging on to the bars with their knees?"

Dan could remember nothing that sounded like the word "circus," and he didn't have any idea what a trapeze was. "No," he said quietly, shaking his head.

"I know you can do this, son," said "Father" encouragingly. "Swing your legs toward the tree itself, toward the center of the tree."

Dan waited a minute and then tried to do what he was told. His right shoe hit the wood but he swung back out again.

"O.K.," said "Father." "That doesn't quite get us where we want. Here's a choice, Dan. Would you rather fall toward me feet first or head first?"

Dan didn't think much of either idea. He tried to shrug, but his shoulders and arms were tiring. He looked down at "Father."

"We're only about ten feet apart, son," said Mr. Knox, smiling up at him. "If you want to, you can just let go and drop, and I'll catch you."

Dan examined his likely fall. Just below his feet was another branch. He would hit it. What would happen then?

"You have to try, son," coached "Father." "Otherwise, you'll have to stay there until I can go to get help."

"I can't," Dan said in a whisper. "I'm going to fall."

Mr. Knox moved slightly away from the tree, to better gauge what might happen. "All right," he said after a moment. "Come ahead. Fall. The worst thing that can happen is that you hit that lower branch. If you do, Dan, just grab it with your hands or your legs. Do you understand?"

Dan did, but he doubted.

"If you hit it with your legs, wrap them around the branch and hang on. You'll be swinging upside down, but you'll be close enough maybe for me to get to you."

Sitting at the junction of two branches above for an hour, Dan had felt safe and secure. Now all he felt was fear. Long ago he had seen barn cats scampering across the tops of houses, up trees, down poles. But he also recalled how some of these cats had suddenly frozen. They had reached a certain place in a tree, or on a ledge of a building, and then decided that that was as far as they could go. Other people had had to climb up to rescue them.

He closed his eyes. He breathed deeply a couple of times. He had nothing to lose.

He let go of his branch.

It happened so quickly, Dan couldn't even picture it in his mind later.

He had begun to fall. He *had* hit the branch below. His right leg had landed on the limb and somehow he had managed to tighten his muscles. Without thinking what he was doing, Dan had stopped his fall and was hanging on to the branch with one leg and both hands.

"Put the other leg over, Dan," shouted Mr. Knox from below.

Which is exactly what Dan had done.

"Good boy!" "Father" said, reaching up to grab hold of a branch below. The limb held him, although it trembled. "Now, Dan, let go of your hands."

"What?"

"Let your hands go. You'll be hanging there, upside down for just a second. I can reach your hands then. Really I can, son. Come on, let go. Let go!"

Dan got a faceful of pine needles as he did what "Father" wanted. And then he felt "Father's" strong grip.

"I've got you, son," said Mr. Knox. "You can let go with your legs now."

He could feel his body being stretched between "Father" and the limb of the tree around which his legs were wrapped. He pulled one leg up and off the limb, his head pointed down toward the rocks around the tree. He closed his eyes.

In midair Dan did a cartwheel.

"Father" caught him and lowered him to the ground with speed and a smoothness that shocked Dan when he realized he was on solid land.

Part II

11

As Dan and his father walked up toward the main road to-gether, hand in hand, Dan had some questions. "What's a circus?" he asked as they climbed a slight rise.

"A circus? Why, that's one of the most exciting shows you'll ever see, Dan. As a matter of fact, one comes through our town every spring. We'll go next time."

"But what is it?"

Dan's father smiled, remembering. "It has lions and tigers and elephants in it, trained ones, although they're never really tame. And clowns and pretty girls on horse-back. And trapeze artists who—"

"What's 'trapeze'? What do those people do?"

"They do just exactly what you did, son!" said Father. "They hang from crossbars, like the branches of a tree, only it's swinging on a wire, very fast, higher and higher. And then, when they judge the time is right, as you did, they let go of the bar, the trapeze, and fly through the air toward each other. A 'catcher' grabs the other person's hands, or wrists, perhaps, and then together the two of them swing high above the floor of the circus, back and forth."

"Do they ever come down?"

"Sure they do," laughed Mr. Knox. "Or they stay up and do more tricks. They have platforms way up high in the rigging, in the wires near the top of the tent, and sometimes a catcher will swing very close to one of these and let go, and his partner, or rider, will just sail through the air to land on it."

"I'd like to see that!" Dan exclaimed.

"We'll go, then, next spring, just the two of us."

"Oh, thank goodness!" cried Mrs. Knox as she came running from the van toward them.

Mr. Knox and Dan stopped where they were, and Mrs. Knox nearly knocked Dan down, she was so eager to hold him. "We didn't know, Dan," she began. "We were so worried . . ."

Mary Kate followed her mother down the hillside at a distance, looking as though she had just had a new idea, and that it pleased her.

"As a psychologist," Mary Kate said almost under her breath, for in the other room Dan and Mr. Knox were still finishing the breakfast that had been put on hold while the search for Dan took place, "you don't think there was a message in all this?"

Mrs. Knox stopped buttering more toast and looked sharply at her daughter.

"Well, dear," she said slowly, "I'd say that Dan was frightened we were going to take him back to the state home and leave him there. It is in the capital and he heard us talking about stopping by to show the building to him. It's probably the most natural thing in the world, I'd say, with Dan's background, to hear something like that and be convinced that he was being rejected."

"Try again," Mary Kate suggested.

"What do you mean?"

"What I mean is this. You don't suppose, just for a minute anyway, Dan was sending a message different from that? Like, hey, I've done this, and now I've decided *I* don't want to live with *them*. Like, hey, I don't want to stay here."

"Would that have pleased you, dear?"

Mary Kate turned away quickly and manufactured a

laugh. "It hasn't anything to do with me, Mother. All I'm suggesting is that maybe there was more to this than you think."

"Hold your thought," commanded her mother as she passed Mary Kate carrying a plate of freshly buttered toast to the dining room. When she came back, she pulled the swinging door behind her closed and stood examining her daughter.

"Are we talking mother-daughter issues here, Mary Kate?"

Mary Kate reddened but threw up her hands in disgust. "It hasn't anything to do with us, for Pete's sake! I'm talking about what Dan wants. Maybe he's more comfortable doing what he has been doing all this time, moving around, I mean. You heard what Dad said. If Dan doesn't want to stay with us, we can't make him."

12

"She just won't listen to me!" Mary Kate complained to her friend Charlotte Gamble. They were at Charlotte's home, a few blocks from the Knox house, in Charlotte's room, examining the state of the world. "Oh, she listens, but as she likes to say about other people all the time, she's listening but she isn't *hearing*."

Charlotte was as light as Mary Kate was dark: blond, blue-eyed, with skin that was so fair a passing sunbeam would make a streak on it. "I don't get it," she said, all smiles. "What is it you want her to hear?"

"Oh, for goodness' sake, haven't you been listening? Who knows if this kid wants to stay with us?"

"But you said he had been adopted."

Mary Kate nodded angrily. "Which just makes it worse. I mean, I don't think you can un-adopt anybody, do you?"

"I don't know," Charlotte answered. "It seems to me that if you, or your family, go to all the trouble of getting Dan, the last thing you'd want to do is give him up."

"Ohhh!" Mary Kate breathed. "Honestly, Charlotte, I'm not getting through to you. Who needs an adopted child if you've already got one of your own and a second on the way?"

Charlotte's normally clear brow furrowed. She thought a minute.

"Well?" prompted Mary Kate.

Charlotte finally shrugged.

"Nobody!" Mary Kate answered her own question. "No one in their right mind."

Charlotte laughed. "You sure couldn't say your mother isn't in her right mind!"

"I imagine psychologists can be just as crazy as anybody else."

"So, what do you want to do?" wondered Charlotte.

Mary Kate sighed. "I don't know. I mean, I do, of course, know what I want. I just can't put it into words."

"That sure doesn't help convince your mother of anything."

"It was my father who said it first!"

"Still . . ."

"You don't know what it's like, Charlotte, having this little dark cloud shadowing you every day. Really. The things that should make him happy, the things that would make any little boy happy, just don't!"

Charlotte rolled over on her stomach, her legs bent up at the knees and her head held off the covers by her hands. "Maybe they will, in time," she offered, reaching out across the mattress to continue reading about Hermione.

"I doubt it," said Mary Kate from the floor nearby, lying on her side. "I really do. I just wish I could talk to Mother about this as easily as I do to you."

Charlotte smiled to herself, pleased at the compliment. "Have you tried?"

"Not yet," said Mary Kate. "Not yet. The time isn't right."

13

"Mother" said she was too exhausted to cook, and Mrs. Farrow had left nothing prepared that could be warmed. When Mr. Knox came home from work, his wife—to the delight of Mary Kate—flirted with him and convinced him that a night out would be a rest and a treat for everyone.

Mary Kate ran upstairs to put on a skirt, and Dan was instructed to change his trousers and put on a sweater.

The family arrived at the restaurant at about seven o'clock. Mr. Knox had telephoned in advance to make a reservation for four. They were shown to their table and were just settling in—Mary Kate's and Dan's eyes big with interest as menus were handed to them—when another man and his wife passed their table. "George!" said the man, slowing his pace.

Mr. Knox stood at his place immediately and extended his hand. "Fred," he said, shaking Fred's hand. "And Evelyn. Nice to see you."

Evelyn smiled down at the table and winked at Mrs. Knox.

"I don't believe you've met our entire family," said Mr. Knox then, still on his feet.

"Well, we can certainly see some of it growing," laughed Evelyn. Mrs. Knox laughed softly, too.

"This is my daughter, Mary Kate," said Mr. Knox. "And this is our son, Dan. This is Evelyn and Fred Farmer."

"Well, he's sure a chip off your block!" said Fred Farmer.

Dan wasn't certain what he should do, so he decided to copy Father. He stood, pushing back his chair, and offered his hand. Fred took it and shook it firmly. "Nice to meet you, Dan," he said. "Your old dad here's a classmate of mine from way back. Why, we grew up in the same neighborhood. We couldn't have been much more than your age when we met."

Mary Kate waited for attention to be turned her way.

Dan couldn't think of what to say, but he nodded and stayed on his feet.

"He's polite as can be," Evelyn noticed out loud. "And cute, too!"

Dan blushed.

"Well, it's certainly nice to see you all," said Fred, gently putting his hand in the small of his wife's back to start her moving away to their own table. "We ought to get together sometime. You play golf, Dan?"

Mr. Knox laughed with surprise. Dan had no idea what Fred Farmer was saying. He sat back down in his chair as the Farmers moved on.

"Nice people," Mr. Knox said as he resumed sitting.

Mary Kate's face said they weren't as nice as all that.

In school, Dan found himself thinking.

It was there he did most of his deep thinking because when he was at "home," he felt too keyed up by having always to watch and listen and adjust and try to guess what was expected of him.

He felt closer to Father, after their adventure at the lake, than anyone else. He didn't doubt "Mother's" affection or good intentions, but she—a little like Mary Kate—was too often busy with other things for the kind of feeling Dan had long dreamed of. Part of this, he knew, was because she was going to have a baby soon.

He had seen other women waiting for the same event,

and sometimes, he recalled, they ignored almost everything except how they felt, and whether or not the baby would be healthy when it arrived. His own place in their lives would grow smaller and smaller as the day of birth arrived. When it did finally come, he became almost invisible.

And then, although he had never before made the connection, he was on his way back to the capital.

Dan sat at his desk, doodling while looking out the window at nothing in particular. Ms. Breeze was talking about something—subtraction, whatever that was—and she seemed to be content with the behavior in her class. When she would stop to ask a question, the question was rarely asked of Dan.

So he thought, about a lot of things.

What could he do to stop being sent back when the baby came?

He realized that in a very short time he had come to like living with the Knoxes. And he was wild about the lakeside cabin. It was too bad the whole family didn't live there all the time.

It was farther from the capital.

The problem, as he saw it, was that there was almost nothing he could do for "Mother" to help her get ready for the baby. There was no way to prove his value to her after the baby came. As before, he would be told he was too small to hold a child, too small to feed it or diaper it or really do much of anything except admire it from a safe distance.

He knew Mary Kate expected the baby to be a girl. More than expected, she almost insisted on it. He himself didn't care what it was. The end result would be the same. He would be frozen out of the Knoxes' life, out of their house.

He sat staring at the front of his classroom, seeing but not paying attention to what was going on. When the bell sounded for the end of day, he had just had a terrific idea. Since he and Father were friends now, maybe he could do what he had done at dinner when he first came: ask. Come right out and talk about what worried him. Father would understand, just as he had earlier, that Dan was afraid, still, of the same thing as before.

"Dan?"

He blinked. Children around him were on their feet, getting their jackets, leaving the classroom. Ms. Breeze was still standing at the front of the room, in front of the blackboard.

"Yes, ma'am?"

"Is your mother outside waiting for you?"

"She will be," said Mary Kate from the doorway.

Ms. Breeze turned and smiled at Mary Kate. "Do you think she could come in for a minute or two? I'd like to talk with her."

Mary Kate's smile and nod were more than merely polite; they were eager. She turned quickly and disappeared.

"Dan, why don't you come up and sit near the desk?" Ms. Breeze suggested.

Dan moved forward as his teacher suggested. He sat in the second row. Ms. Breeze smiled at him.

"How are you settling in, Dan?" she asked after a moment.

Dan nodded shyly. "O.K."

"Making friends?"

Dan thought of Brian Baldwin. "A few."

"Good," said his teacher. "That's part of what school is for, meeting new people. Learning how to make friends, sharing happy times."

Dan nodded again, a terrible feeling growing in the pit of his stomach. Why was he being held after class? Why did "Mother" have to come in? What was the rule he had broken?

"Hello, Frances," said Mrs. Knox as she preceded her daughter into the classroom. "How are you?"

Dan's teacher smiled warmly. "I'm fine, Doctor. Sometimes I surprise even myself."

"Well, you look wonderful," said Mrs. Knox, ruffling the hair at the top of Dan's head as she passed. She put her purse on a desk in front of his, and sat down in its chair. Dan looked quickly around to see Mary Kate planted near the doorway. He didn't like the look on her face.

"The reason I wanted to talk with you," said Ms. Breeze, settling into her own chair behind her desk, "is Dan."

Dan froze.

"I imagined that," said "Mother." "The week we took off. Did that put him behind?"

Ms. Breeze shook her head and smiled.

"Well, that's good," said Mrs. Knox. "We did a lot of reading up at the cabin," she offered.

Dan looked again at Mary Kate. From a distance, he couldn't see whether she was breathing. But the light in her eyes was clear as she inched forward just a bit to hear better.

"Dan isn't really . . ." Ms. Breeze paused, as though searching for the right words. "Well, he just hasn't joined the class yet, I guess."

"I don't understand," said Mrs. Knox. "He's here every day."

"Yes, I know. Maybe I wasn't too clear. He's here in body, but not in spirit."

"He's not causing any disruption?" asked Mrs. Knox quickly.

Dan held his breath. He didn't know what the word meant, but he sensed it wasn't good.

"Not at all. He's very well behaved. Quiet. Reflective." Ms. Breeze folded her hands, one atop the other, and leaned forward. "He's so reflective, Doctor, that I suspect very little of what we do here is reaching him."

Dan was still puzzled by the words being used, but he became cold just the same. There was something being said that he thought wasn't what "Mother" would want to hear. He had always sort of liked Ms. Breeze. Suddenly he wondered whether he had been wrong. Maybe she had the power to do what other grown-ups could.

Mrs. Knox turned in her chair and reached behind her for one of Dan's hands. He let her take it. She turned back toward his teacher.

"You know, Frances, Dan is a very watchful young man."

Ms. Breeze nodded in agreement. "Guarded, I would say."

"You could," Mrs. Knox said. "But as you know, he has a lot of very good reasons to hold back."

"Yes, I can see that," said Dan's teacher. "And I wonder what experiences he had before, in school."

"They weren't too stable," said Mrs. Knox. "I would guess he was allowed to go infrequently. He was usually doing so many other things."

Ms. Breeze nodded again. "Still, we need him to join us here, don't we, if he's to come along the learning trail."

Mrs. Knox agreed quickly. "Of course. And I appreciate your insight, Frances, I really do. And later Dan will, too. I think if we give him a little more time . . ."

"We will, Doctor. I merely wanted to say he's not yet part of our class here, our studies. He dreams a good deal. You can see him move in and out of the present, and that seems to make him comfortable. I'm glad that it does. But he needs to pay more attention to what's in front of him."

Mrs. Knox stood up, letting go of Dan's hand. She put one of her own hands on her stomach. "We all are rather preoccupied, as you can imagine."

Ms. Breeze laughed softly. "I don't wonder. I just didn't want Dan to miss some of the fundamentals he'll need later in life."

Mrs. Knox nodded at Dan, who stood up. "Frances, I wish every teacher were as alert as you are. It's very good of you to take the time to worry over Dan like this."

"He's a nice boy."

Dan sighed deep inside. Whatever had been going on was O.K. now. He could tell by the tones of voice being used. He looked over his shoulder at Mary Kate, and was surprised to see, rather than a smile of relief like the one he felt, a frown of disappointment

"You had to stay in?" Brian Baldwin asked from behind his fence. "Well, nobody gets to take a week off just for fun. People do in the winter, but not now!"

"It wasn't so bad," Dan reported.

"What did she want?"

Dan shrugged. "Just to talk, to my 'mother.'"

"Do you like her? Ms. Breeze, I mean."

Dan shrugged. "I don't know."

"I guess I kind of do," Brian allowed. "She's old and alone and all she has is us."

"Who told you that?"

"Well, you can see for yourself," Brian explained. "She's as old as my folks, and she doesn't wear a wedding ring."

"That doesn't mean she's lonely," Dan said.

There was a moment of silence then.

"What have you been exposed to?" Brian Baldwin asked quietly.

Dan didn't hear the question clearly. His mind was still on his teacher at school. "What?"

"My mom says you've been exposed to things," Brian said. "What kinds of things?"

"What's 'exposed'?" asked Dan.

Brian shrugged behind the fence.

Dan waited for Brian's answer. Hearing nothing, he moved up close to the pickets and tried to peer through at his friend. "How come you hide behind the fence?" he asked. "I mean, we see each other every day at school. How come you hide now?"

"I'm not hiding!" Brian answered quickly.

"Well, what would you call it?"

"I'm not allowed," Brian said.

"Not allowed to do what?"

"Not allowed to go into your yard, or play with you." Dan backed away from the fence.

"You've been exposed," Brian repeated.

"What does that mean?"

"I don't know," Brian admitted. "But my mother says that children like you have been exposed to all kinds of things."

"I still don't get it," Dan said, frustrated.

"I think 'exposed' means you've been close to something, like measles or chicken pox."

"I haven't!"

"It was just an example."

"Well, so what if I had?" Dan challenged. "Lots of people are."

"My mom thinks you might be a bad influence on me," Brian said very quietly.

"What does *that* mean?"

"She says children like you have a lot of problems," Brian said gently, trying hard not to make his friend angry. "I don't agree with her, but that's what she says. She says foster children get into a lot of trouble."

Dan stood still, thinking. He didn't think he *was* a foster child anymore. He was about to say this, but before he could speak, he heard his name being called.

He turned around. Mary Kate was standing in the kitchen doorway.

"What?" he called back.

"I've got a surprise for you. Come on in."

Dan looked back at the fence where Brian was. "Go ahead," said his friend. "I'll see you tomorrow."

Dan nodded and pulled up his collar. Autumn had arrived.

14

"I don't see how you can stand the cold," Mary Kate said, smiling broadly as she closed the door behind Dan.

"It's not so bad," said Dan. He was a little suspicious of his "sister."

"I made you some cocoa," Mary Kate announced proudly, pointing to the center table on which stood a steaming mug of the stuff, and a plate of chocolate chip cookies.

Dan stood a moment without moving. "That's nice."

"Well, go ahead. Try it," Mary Kate urged, her hand on Dan's shoulder pushing him in that direction.

Dan let himself be guided. He sat down and lifted the mug. The scent from the cup was warm and sweet.

He was startled when Mary Kate sat down beside him.

"We really haven't spent much time together," Mary Kate said pleasantly. "Talking, I mean."

Dan sipped the drink.

"You must have had a really interesting life, before you got here."

"Why?"

"Well, because. Because you got to meet so many different people. I mean, wherever you went."

"You mean because I've been 'exposed'?"

Mary Kate seemed puzzled for a moment, but she held her smile.

Dan waited to hear what she would say about his being exposed. From the way Brian talked, being exposed was clearly a bad thing. Something that only happened to children like himself.

"I just mean you've had a lot of experiences," Mary Kate said after a moment. "For instance, where did you live before you came here?"

Dan's face betrayed nothing. There was something almost threatening, he thought, about Mary Kate's questions. She had never before been nice to him. She hadn't been mean, really, either, just uninterested. What was all this about?

She leaned forward toward him, still smiling in a welcoming way. "Well?"

"You know," Dan said.

"I don't mean the institution," Mary Kate explained. "I mean, who were the people you lived with before us?"

Dan didn't like the question.

"Were they . . . what? Farmers or city people like us, or . . . ?"

"Scott," Dan said suddenly. "That was their name. Scott."

Mary Kate grinned. "Were they nice people?"

"No. . . . Sometimes."

"Well, there, you see. You know, you've probably seen more of the grown-up world than I have."

Dan imagined this was so, but said nothing.

"Where did they live?"

"On a farm."

"Terrific! That must have been great, being outdoors all the time and being around . . . well, horses and cows and chickens and things."

Dan took another tiny sip of his chocolate.

"Did you have fun there?"

Dan looked into Mary Kate's face. He couldn't see anything but curiosity. "No."

"Why? Were they mean to you?"

"I have to go upstairs now," Dan announced, standing up, unzipping his jacket.

Mary Kate sat at the table, smiling to herself.

Dan stood at his window, looking out onto the front yard and the driveway.

What could he have been "exposed" to, besides what Brian mentioned? He tried to think back, to remember, but most of his life so far was cloudy. There were so many things he had purposely tried to forget.

Idly he wondered at what age people started to remember their lives.

He could think back maybe a year or two. He could count four families he knew he had stayed with for different periods of time. And he could remember being returned to the state four times. As far as he knew, each journey back to the capital had been because he had forgotten rules.

He watched the outside light dim, and streetlights blink on. Houses across the way also began to be lit.

This was the nicest neighborhood Dan could remember living in. True, he was still somewhat in the dark about the Knox family rules, but maybe this family didn't have so many.

He closed his eyes then, trying to remember what he had been told in his new home. The only thing that came to his mind was that everyone's room could only be entered after someone asked permission. But there had to have been others, signals perhaps he had missed along the way.

He didn't hear the door to his room being opened carefully. He didn't hear the footsteps behind him. He wasn't aware of someone's breath at his shoulder.

"You don't have to stay here, you know," whispered Mary Kate into his right ear.

Dan jumped, and turned. "What?"

Mary Kate was standing inches away from him, looking down at him, smiling in a horrible fake way. "I said, you don't have to stay if you don't want to."

"Why wouldn't I want to?"

Mary Kate shrugged. "I just remember the lake, when you disappeared. I thought maybe you were telling us you wanted to be by yourself."

Dan couldn't think what to say in reply.

"After all," Mary Kate added, "there's a lot to be said for being on your own. There's freedom, for one thing. You get to do what you want when you want to. You get to make the choices every day. Doesn't that sound great?"

Dan turned away from Mary Kate and looked out into the darkness.

"You've had a lot of experience," she whispered softly. "You should put it to good use."

"Why are you saying this?" Dan asked in a small voice, still looking out the window as though hypnotized.

"Maybe I'm the only one who can understand," Mary Kate offered delicately. "We're not so far apart in age as the others."

Dan said nothing.

"Think how easy it would be to just walk out of here, walk down the street, and start life on your own. No rules, no one telling you what to do, no one forcing you to go anywhere, to go back."

Dan saw a car enter the driveway below. His father's. Its headlights bounced at the curb and hit the front of the house below the window where he stood.

When he turned around finally, Mary Kate had disappeared.

15

Mrs. Farrow's car was where "Mother's" usually was. Dan stopped in his tracks.

"Come on," insisted Mary Kate.

"What is she doing here?"

Mary Kate pulled Dan's arm. "We'll find out. Come on!"

When they got to the car, Mary Kate opened her door and Dan pulled open the door to Mrs. Farrow's backseat. He had barely climbed in before he heard Mary Kate.

"What's going on?" she asked eagerly. "Is Mom . . . ?"

Mrs. Farrow smiled. "Yes, she is. Your father's already been called. I just dropped her off at the hospital."

"Oh, that's wonderful!" Mary Kate cried. "Let's go!"

"Not to the hospital," Mrs. Farrow announced, pulling her car away from the school curb.

"Why not?" asked Mary Kate.

Mrs. Farrow smiled to herself. "This is a time for your parents to be together. Later, afterward, you and Dan can go visit."

"But why can't we go now?" Mary Kate demanded.

"You can't, miss," said Mrs. Farrow. "That's all there is to it."

Mary Kate sank down into her seat. Dan couldn't see her face but he knew she wasn't happy.

And he wasn't, either. This was the beginning of the end. He knew it. In a few weeks he would be back where he began, trying to explain to other kids why he had been returned.

He hadn't guessed all this could happen so quickly.

Mary Kate's face had turned pale. "What do you mean?" she asked her father. "What complications?"

Mr. Knox took off his tie and pulled the sweater Mrs. Farrow handed him over his head. He replaced his glasses on the end of his nose.

Dan was standing motionlessly near the back of a big chair.

"Well, you know, sweetheart, having a baby isn't always easy," said Mr. Knox.

"People do it all the time!" Mary Kate objected.

"Some people do it more easily than others," explained her father. "And when you are an older woman, as your mother is, well, sometimes your flexibility isn't what it was when you were younger."

"Flexibility?" Mary Kate asked.

"Never mind, Mary Kate. All I'm saying is that this is taking longer than we had thought, and that there might be some medical problems along the way we hadn't foreseen."

Mary Kate spun in frustration, her voice rising. "This is the twenty-first century!" she announced. "We've got X rays and tests and medicines for everything! How can there be any surprises?"

Mr. Knox grinned, but not really happily. "Life is like this, Mary Kate. Modern science can't solve every problem."

He looked at Mrs. Farrow, who seemed to understand what his glance meant. She left the room and returned a second later with a heavy jacket, which she handed to him.

"All you two have to do," said Mr. Knox, putting one arm through a sleeve, "is stay here with Mrs. Farrow, have a wonderful dinner and get some rest. I'm sure by tomorrow, maybe even before you go to bed tonight, everything will have worked out."

"Will you call us?" asked Mary Kate.

"If there's time," replied her father. "If there's news."

"What kind of baby is it going to be?" asked Dan then, his voice uncertain.

Mr. Knox walked to where Dan stood and picked him up. "One of two kinds," he said confidently. "A boy, or a girl."

"But I thought you knew!" Mary Kate exploded.

Mr. Knox hugged Dan and set him on the floor. "The doctors do, sweetheart. But your mother and I wanted to be surprised. After all, having another child itself is a surprise. All we wanted to hear was that the baby is healthy. And it is," he said, kissing the top of Mary Kate's head as he started for the door that led into the garage. "Now, mind Mrs. Farrow, and get to bed early."

"But—"

Mr. Knox pulled open the door and then turned to look at his daughter. "It will be one or the other, Mary Kate. What matters is getting your mother through this. Be helpful. Stay calm."

Dan liked Mrs. Farrow. When his father's car had backed out of the drive, when the garage door had fallen almost silently into place, it was to her side that he went. He didn't trust Mary Kate.

Mrs. Farrow put her hand on Dan's shoulder and squeezed it gently. "Don't you worry, Dan," she offered quietly. "Everything'll be fine." She patted him on the back. "So, now, what would you two like for dinner?"

"I couldn't dream of eating," Mary Kate announced dramatically. With a quick glare at Dan, she whirled and walked out of the room to go upstairs.

Dan was aflame with thoughts. Each new one made him turn red with joy and then white with fear.

Whatever he asked to eat tonight could very well be one of his last meals at the Knoxes'. Who cared about the baby, whether it was a boy or a girl? The end result of its arrival would be his dismissal.

But—and here inwardly he shouted encouragement to himself—why not Mrs. Farrow? She seemed to like him. No, he was certain she did. Why couldn't she take him in?

It wasn't so far-fetched. She was a part, almost, of the Knox family. She had a car. She could help him pack and drive him back to wherever she lived. He would be able to stay in the same school, maybe.

He wouldn't have to think about the capital.

And he had already told her the many things he could do to help her. All he would have to do was find out *her* rules, and follow them.

"A big juicy hamburger," Mrs. Farrow decided. "Come on, sonny boy. We'll build a burger so big you won't be able to see over it."

Dan nodded and smiled and tagged in Mrs. Farrow's

footsteps to the kitchen. This would be a great time to show how helpful he could be.

Mary Kate held out until nearly eight o'clock before she descended in silence and made herself an ice-cream sundae in the kitchen. Dan and Mrs. Farrow were in front of the television set, watching a Disney movie.

Mary Kate walked into the den holding her bowl of ice cream and leaned against the doorway. "How can you two be so selfish?" she wondered aloud. "Mother may die tonight!"

Mrs. Farrow turned her head quickly to look at Mary Kate, ignoring the drama Mary Kate was manufacturing. "I don't think that's likely, Mary Kate," she said.

"You heard Daddy. He just wasn't telling us the whole truth."

Dan stared at the screen, afraid to turn around to look at Mary Kate.

"He was," argued Mrs. Farrow. "Don't get all actressy now," she cautioned. "Your mother will be fine. And so will the baby."

"Grown-ups want us to believe everything they say," Mary Kate replied angrily, "when they know half of it is just bananas."

"This grown-up is telling you the truth, dear," Mrs. Farrow said sharply. "Now, instead of trying to frighten us all, or scolding us, why don't you just sit down, get comfortable, and watch the movie?"

"I couldn't," Mary Kate sighed. "I just couldn't."

"Then go to bed," Mrs. Farrow suggested.

"It's too early."

Dan thought he would like to go to bed and hide.

"Well, what time does Your Highness have in mind?"

Mary Kate posed a moment. "If Daddy isn't back by ten, then, maybe, I'll *try* to sleep."

"Fair enough," Mrs. Farrow decided. "In the meantime, if you can't be cheerful, go play on your computer or read or do something useful."

"No," Mary Kate said thoughtfully. "I'll wait here with you till ten. I'll wait till Dan goes up, too."

Dan wasn't happy at that prospect. He nestled more closely into Mrs. Farrow's side.

Mr. Knox telephoned from the hospital. He told Mrs. Farrow he would be staying the night there, that Mrs. Knox was coming along fine but that the baby hadn't arrived yet. How were the children?

Mrs. Farrow assured him that Mary Kate and Dan were fine, that they had eaten and were almost ready for bed. She herself, she said, would sleep in Mrs. Knox's office.

When the conversation was ended, Mary Kate stood up from her chair. "He didn't ask to speak to us?" she wondered.

"I imagine he has a lot on his mind," Mrs. Farrow said. "Now then, it's nearly ten. Let's do the best we can and try to get some rest."

Dan slid off the couch and started for the stairway. "Wait a minute!" Mrs. Farrow called to him. "Don't I get a hug?"

Dan was happy to do what she wanted. This was a good new rule.

Then he marched upstairs, brushed his teeth, and put on his pajamas. As he went to his doorway to turn out the overhead light, he was startled to find Mary Kate standing just outside in the hall.

"We need to talk," she advised him.

"About what?"

"You."

Mary Kate strode into the room, not smiling. She threw herself atop Dan's bed and looked severely at him. He still stood by his doorway.

"Well," she said, "come in and close the door."

"Why should I close the door?"

"So we can talk, for heaven's sake!"

Then Mary Kate smiled—an enormous, welcoming, warm smile that Dan didn't believe for one minute. He did close the door, but he held on to its handle.

"We have a little problem, Dan," she began, her smile thinning just a bit.

Dan waited, saying nothing.

"If Mother survives and we have a new baby, there isn't going to be a lot of time to pay attention to you."

Mary Kate couldn't have known the length of the lance she had just hurled into Dan's stomach. But he did not flinch. He waited.

"Think about it," Mary Kate advised. "I mean, it would be different if you'd been here forever, or if you were my real brother. But you're not. And everyone will be focusing on the baby, which is perfectly natural, you know. Babies are so fragile."

Dan knew all this. He was breathing somewhat easier, but he was also, just a little, beginning to get angry.

"When you think back," Mary Kate continued, "to the other families where you've stayed, surely there's one you liked, one you sort of actually miss. Isn't there?"

Dan shook his head. "No," he said very quietly.

"What about the Scotts, on the farm? Or the people before that?"

"Nope."

"Well, someone must have loved you, treated you well."

Dan just stared at Mary Kate.

"Anyway," she bulled on, "it's just like what Daddy said. We can't make you stay here unless you want to."

"He said that?"

"At the lake, when you were hiding."

Dan considered this a moment. That was before he and Father had done the circus trick together. He might have said that, but he might really have been worried about it, too. Dan wanted to believe this.

"Do you?" Mary Kate pressed. "Want to stay, I mean. No matter what? Even with the baby?"

Dan couldn't decide what to say. If he said yes, Mary Kate would be angrier than ever. If he said no, she would tell "Mother" and Father, and then where would he be? Inwardly he knew. He hated the idea.

"Even if I warned you against staying?" Mary Kate challenged. "Even if I told you I would do everything I could to see you leave here?"

"Yes!"

Mary Kate's eyes widened and the tiny smile that had lingered on her lips faded completely.

"Yes," Dan said again. "I would. I will."

Mary Kate waited a moment before she stood up. "You've been warned."

Part III

16

Sleep that night did not come easily to Dan.

He was angry. He was frightened. He was determined. He was sad.

What had he done to make Mary Kate feel this way about him? He had done his best to stay out of her way. Failing that, he had always been nice to her. Nearly from his first day, he had known she was mean, no matter how she smiled and talked nicely about him in front of "Mother" and Father.

Well, he wasn't going to be bullied by her. She wasn't

a grown-up. She couldn't do what other grown-ups had done. She might not like him, but he felt that "Mother" and Father did. He hoped they did.

He was almost sure they did.

As for the baby coming, there wasn't much he could do about that except watch and wait, and stay awake to every opportunity he had to show how good he could be with it, how willing he was to work hard to make "Mother's" life easier.

He could avoid Mary Kate. He would avoid Mary Kate. She would, after all, have to make up things to say about him. And when she did, he could deny them, argue them away.

The only problem was that Mary Kate was a real Knox and he wasn't. If someone had to choose whom to believe, wouldn't they choose the older person, the one they'd known longest, a real part of the family?

He thought once more of how Father had caught him when he fell from the tree at the lakeside. Whenever he needed to brighten his spirits, he thought of this.

Imagining his father's hands catching him, feeling again that strength, he felt not just safe from Mary Kate but hopeful.

And as long as he had hope, he would fight. It was worth it. He was tired of being pushed around.

*   *   *

After breakfast the next day, Mrs. Farrow told Mary Kate and Dan to put on their jackets. There was enough time to get to the hospital to visit their mother before going to school. Although, she said, and she stressed this firmly, the visit couldn't be a long one. They would be at the hospital hours before regular visiting time began, and so they had to slip in and out as quietly as possible.

"Do you know her room number?" asked Mary Kate as she got into Mrs. Farrow's car.

"109," was the reply.

Dan sat in the backseat drowning in his own thoughts. He was still going to fight to stay, but would he have help? Would "Mother" and Father really be too busy for him, as Mary Kate had said? Was this the beginning of his trip back to the capital? What could he do once he saw "Mother" to plead with her not to send him away?

He had not said a word to Mary Kate all morning. She had told him how she felt, and he had done the same. There really wasn't more either of them could say. When their eyes met, each looked quickly somewhere else. Dan felt like he was at war.

Mrs. Farrow's car pulled into the emergency parking lot, passed through it, and came to a stop at an angle in the regular visitors' lot. Mary Kate was first out, and walked quickly toward the hospital's front doors. She walked determinedly ahead of Dan and Mrs. Farrow, with her shoulders back and her chin forward, important and needed.

By the time Dan and Mrs. Farrow entered the hospital, Mary Kate had read signs and was off and running down a corridor ahead of them. She disappeared around a corner. Mrs. Farrow and Dan followed at a gentler pace, hand in hand.

Dan had never before been in a hospital. There had been times in his life when he recalled people saying he should go to one, should be taken to one. But always a decision was made for him: he was brave, he could recover, who could afford the expense? His eyes were wide as he walked along, looking at lighted signs above doorways, seeing arrows pointing in one direction or another, hearing tiny bells signal in the distance some need or name.

He and Mrs. Farrow came to the closed door of room 109. Mrs. Farrow looked down into Dan's face with a smile. "Well, go on ahead," she urged. "Your family's waiting."

She pushed open the door for him and then stood back to make certain he entered the room first.

He looked past the back of his father's figure to see Mary Kate at the bedside. She was glowing with happiness. His eyes moved only slightly to see "Mother" lying in bed, something in a pink blanket held close. That must be the baby. "Mother" saw Dan and smiled hugely. He took another step into the room, followed by Mrs. Farrow.

"It's a girl!" Mary Kate announced happily. "I knew it. I knew it would be a girl!"

"Thanksgiving will have a new meaning for us all, won't it?" said Mr. Knox.

"Come up here, Dan," said "Mother." "Don't you want to say hello to her? She's here just a trifle early. We thought she would arrive closer to Christmas."

Dan looked quickly at his father for reassurance. He edged toward the bed.

"No, darling," said "Mother." "I meant jump up here, with me."

Dan put his foot on the frame beneath the hospital bed and hoisted himself toward "Mother" and the pink bundle. He couldn't imagine how Mary Kate could have known that it would be a girl. He balanced on his knees.

"Mother" lifted the blanketed baby and shifted her to the side closer to Dan. "This is Krista," said "Mother." "Krista Mallory Knox. Say hello, Dan. Shake hands with her."

"I've been exposed," he said, his face reddening.

Mrs. Knox looked quickly at her husband. "To what, dear? We're all exposed to things, and most of them don't matter one bit."

"Who told you that?" asked Father.

"Brian Baldwin."

Mrs. Knox again held out Krista toward Dan. "Mrs. Baldwin is a nice woman, Dan, but she has some very different ideas. You're just fine. Believe me."

Despite his continuing puzzlement, Dan felt a flood of gratitude.

"So, come on, Dan. Shake hands."

Dan was nervous but he reached out a hand. The baby couldn't yet have seen Dan, but something seemed to pass between the two of them, for instinctively she, too, stretched out a tiny hand. Dan put a finger in it and Krista's fingers wrapped around it. Dan couldn't help but let out a little laugh. He was surprised. And he was even more surprised when Krista seemed not to want to let go of his finger.

He looked across the bed. He saw his smiling father standing with his arm around Mary Kate. And he saw a scowling Mary Kate, her dark eyes fixed on his own.

He felt "Mother's" hand on his head, ruffling his hair and pulling him closer to her.

"Oh, Dan," she said softly. "What a family we have."

Dan closed his eyes and laid his head on the covers near Mother, still with Krista's hand around his finger.

He was full of joy. Mary Kate couldn't ruin his life here. Father wouldn't let her. And neither would Mother. He was someone's big brother!

A moment passed.

He kept his eyes closed, content to rest atop the covers with his mother's hand on his head.

17

Mary Kate was silent all the way to school. She never turned around to see or speak to Dan. Instead, she hunched against the passenger door and let Mrs. Farrow gush about the baby.

"It's just the most wonderful thing in the world to have a baby in the house," Mrs. Farrow said, steering her car carefully through early-morning traffic. "The smells and the toys and all. Of course," she laughed, "some of the smells aren't that nice, but you get used to them. But when she's been bathed and powdered and dressed snugly, oh, the scent she gives off. Even today I can remember what each of my kids smelled like when they were fresh and clean."

Dan leaned forward over the seat back. "How did you learn about babies?" he asked. "I mean, to care for them and all?"

"Well, Dan, a good mother just seems to know, by instinct. Something inside her tells her what to do. Something inside helps her recognize when the baby is crying for food or when she's wet or when she's sick. I guess there are books about it, but nothing beats experience."

"Books?" Dan asked. "In a library?"

"Well, I imagine so, dear," said Mrs. Farrow, turning the car toward the curb in front of Mary Kate and Dan's school.

Mary Kate was out of the car with the door slammed behind her before Dan even touched his own handle inside.

"Oh dear," sighed Mrs. Farrow. "Something's up."

"You have a baby brother, don't you?"

Dan and Brian stood together in the center of the playground at recess, both wrapped against the autumn chill.

Brian nodded, his glasses sliding down his nose and then being pushed back up quickly.

"So, what did you do?"

"What do you mean?"

"Well, after the baby came."

Brian shrugged. "Not much. There wasn't much for me to do except look at him."

Dan wasn't surprised at this. But to think that a real child, someone with a real family, was treated as he had been before interested him.

"Did they let you hold him, or touch him, or play with him?"

"How much can you do with a baby?" asked Brian in return. "I mean, they're not really interesting."

Dan waited for more.

"They're cute and all," Brian continued after a moment, shivering just a little. "But they don't *do* anything."

"But they learn," objected Dan. "I thought babies learned from their very first minute."

"Maybe they do, but who can tell? They don't talk. They can hardly see. They sleep a lot and cry a lot and get wet." Brian laughed suddenly. "That's something they do! Charlie peed all over my grandmother!"

"What?"

"I'm serious," Brian added happily. "She was changing him and he just let go. Got her right in the face! If she hadn't been wearing glasses, she'd have been blinded!" He paused. "I don't think girls can do that."

A bell sounded on the playground. Together, hunched against the breeze, the two turned toward school and their classroom.

"Babies aren't really interesting," Brian said. "I mean, not at first. They're not any real trouble. It's when they get older, like Charlie is now, around two, that they get to be sort of fun."

Dan knew he didn't have two years to prove himself.

At the end of the day Mrs. Farrow's car sat at the school curb. Dan saw it and climbed into the backseat automatically.

The minute his door was closed behind him, Mrs. Farrow steered the car into traffic.

"What about Mary Kate?" Dan asked quickly.

"I'll be getting her later, Dan," Mrs. Farrow said, looking into her rearview mirror at Dan. "She called during lunch. She's spending some time with her friend Charlotte."

Dan sat back. "Oh." He had seen Charlotte from a distance. She was pretty and smiled a lot. He didn't think Mary Kate could poison her mind, too, no matter how she tried. But that didn't matter so much as staying alert at home, waiting for whatever it was Mary Kate was planning.

He would have to be on his guard. He would have to, he realized then, shadow Mary Kate wherever she went. He couldn't allow her to have time alone with Mother or Father. Or with Krista, either, now that he thought about it. Who knew how much babies understood?

"When will Mother get home?"

"I think tomorrow, dear," answered Mrs. Farrow. "She's taking a little extra time to rest. Having a baby is hard work."

Dan nodded wisely. "Can we go to the library, please?" he asked.

"I need a book about babies," Dan said seriously to the children's librarian, a pretty woman who sat behind a very well-organized desk.

The young woman's eyebrows rose just a bit. "About what exactly?" she asked. "Where they come from? How they grow?"

"I need a book about how to handle a baby," Dan explained. "What can I do that won't hurt a baby?"

The librarian smiled thoughtfully, and stood up. "Well, let's see what we have here, shall we?"

Dan dutifully followed the woman across a carpeted room, past shelves and small tables and chairs. She knelt down in front of a shelf of books and started fingering them, pulling one out an inch and then slipping it back into its row.

"Well, you know, there's not as much as you'd think," the librarian said to Dan.

"It doesn't have to be a long book," Dan offered. "I don't read all that well. If it had pictures, that would help."

"Here's something that might fit the bill," the librarian said, sliding out from the shelf a picture book whose cover featured a little boy holding a green-blanketed baby.

The young woman stood and carried the book to a round table. She motioned for Dan to take a chair. She opened the book for him. "Why don't you just look through it? When you come to a part that looks interesting, tell me, and we'll read it together."

Dan took the book and turned it over. On the back was a picture of a woman who still had her baby inside her, and the same little boy. He felt doubtful.

The librarian smiled kindly. "I'll be right over there," she explained, pointing back at her desk. "Call me when you need me."

"Thank you," said Dan, turning the book over once more.

When he was alone, Dan opened the book carefully. He began to page through it. He saw a picture of a doctor and a hospital nurse and a scale. He kept going.

There were pictures of the baby *inside* its mother, which Dan wasn't eager to examine. There were pictures of the baby's family at home, getting ready for it. So far there wasn't anything that seemed helpful to him.

He turned more pages. Grandparents. Well, that was nice, but he didn't even know if he had any.

Dan was beginning to lose hope. So far there hadn't

been a picture of the little boy playing with a baby at all. Or holding it, or talking to it, or singing to it, or anything he could imagine himself doing. This was not good.

Finally he came upon a picture in which the baby lay in a basket, with its brother nearby.

Eagerly, he turned the next page.

But everything that followed had to do with *other* people taking care of the baby! Bathing and dressing and feeding seemed work for grown-ups. All the boy in the book did was stand around watching. What good was that?

Finally, near the very end of the book, he saw a picture of the little boy offering something to the baby in the basket. He looked at the page before this, and saw that the baby was crying, and that the boy had discovered a toy that made noise.

Dan didn't need to read the book. He could tell what had happened. The boy had offered the baby the toy that made noise, and the baby stopped crying.

The end.

Dan sat a moment, thinking.

Maybe Brian was right. Maybe what Dan had thought all along was wrong! Maybe there really wasn't much someone like him could do with a baby, for a baby. Maybe—but then he frowned. If that were true, then before, when he had been "cashed in," it really was something he had done.

Dan closed the book. If he combined what Brian had said with what he'd seen in the book, babies didn't really *need* brothers for anything. At least not right away.

These were not happy thoughts.

He leaned back in his small chair. What could he do? And what had he done before that had caused other people with a baby to let him go?

Mr. Knox came home that evening. He looked tired, but he smiled at Dan and Mary Kate. "Your mother and Krista will come home tomorrow," he said. "There's nothing particularly different we need to do, except be a little quiet. The baby needs to sleep, and your mother needs to rest. So we'll all try not to worry her."

Mary Kate nodded as though she agreed entirely, and knew all this anyway. Dan simply sat silently.

"No friends here for a while, Mary Kate," said her father then. "You understand?"

"Of course," Mary Kate agreed.

"Dan, do you have any questions?"

Dan had a dozen, but they were all for Mary Kate, and he couldn't begin to ask them.

18

"You did what?"

Charlotte's mouth was open and her eyes were big. "With Toby Carter? I thought you hated Toby Carter!"

Mary Kate lay on the floor of Charlotte's bedroom. She looked up at her friend. "Well, I do," she admitted. "But I couldn't think of anyone else to help me. He knows so many official-sounding words."

"Oh, Mary Kate!" Charlotte moaned. "How could you?"

"I *had* to!" Mary Kate defended quickly. "How else am I going to get rid of him?"

Charlotte didn't answer the question directly. "I can't believe he's as bad as all that," she said quietly. "I can't think of anything you've told me that's so terrible."

"Well, of course not!" Mary Kate argued. "I mean, how terrible can someone his age be, for heaven's sake!"

"Then why would you—"

"It was the only thing I could think of."

Charlotte closed her eyes. She sat atop her bed cross-legged. "It's not very nice," she said finally.

"Listen, he's used to it," Mary Kate reasoned aloud.

"That makes it even worse!"

Mary Kate shrugged.

"When will all this happen?" asked Charlotte.

"Probably not right away. Everything closes for Thanksgiving, after all. And besides, the people there are probably terrifically busy herding all these kids around. We'll just wait and see."

"How could Toby—"

"On his computer, silly!" Mary Kate explained. "It's really easy. There's nothing on the page that can be traced or even checked."

"Except a signature," Charlotte warned. "I assume someone signed the letter. Someone would have to."

"Someone did," said Mary Kate.

Charlotte looked down at Mary Kate and scowled. "Ohhh, Mary Kate," was what she said.

19

Mrs. Farrow picked Mary Kate and Dan up at school the
next day and drove them home.

Mary Kate leaped from the front seat of the car and
sped toward the house before Dan could think why. He
walked up the path with Mrs. Farrow, hand in hand. Just
as she opened the front door that had been slammed shut,
Dan understood what Mary Kate was doing.

He broke away from Mrs. Farrow and ran, going up
the steps two at a time until he got to the door of his parents' room. This door, too, had been slammed loudly.

He stood a moment, thinking. Mary Kate was behind that door, with his mother and the baby. She was trying to keep him away from both of them.

Dan turned slowly away from the door and started to walk to the top of the steps.

He stopped. The Dan he had been would have slunk away, shut out, worried and unhappy. But not anymore!

The new Dan was going to walk right through that door, and see the baby, too!

Mary Kate had warned him. Well, then, he would warn her. If she wanted war, she'd get it!

He did stop to knock.

"Come in, darling," his mother called.

Dan opened the door slowly and peeked in.

Mary Kate was holding Krista, swinging her a little in her arms, standing next to his mother, who lay in bed. She looked up at Dan with triumph in her eyes. Dan looked away and walked a few more steps into the room.

"Hello, sweetheart," said his mother. "You know, this is the first time all three of you have been home in the same room."

Dan nodded and closed in on Mary Kate, standing on tiptoe to look into her arms.

Krista was wide-eyed and calm. She was wrapped in a pink blanket, and Dan could tell by the size of the bundle

Mary Kate held, she had more clothes on than just the blanket.

"Is she wearing a diaper?" he asked.

"Oh, dear, she'll be in diapers for a long time, I'm afraid," said his mother.

Dan swallowed hard. "May I hold her?"

"No!" said Mary Kate immediately.

His mother smiled at him. "Tomorrow, Dan. We'll let Mary Kate hang on to Krista for a little while longer before we put her down. Then tomorrow can be your turn."

Mary Kate grinned with satisfaction.

Dan could tell what she was thinking. If she got home first again, she'd hold the baby again, and he wouldn't.

"Hey! Not so fast!" called Mrs. Knox as Dan flew past her office and up the stairs.

Dan didn't stop to talk. Mary Kate was right behind him.

But he got to his parents' room first. He dashed into the room and slammed the door shut behind him.

Krista lay in her crib, drowsy but awake. Dan ran to put his hands into the crib to lift her. He had to balance on the wooden frame of the crib in order to reach up and over its safety bar.

"Not that way!" screamed Mary Kate from the doorway. "Hold her head! You could break her neck that way!"

Dan quickly adjusted his arms, holding Krista carefully with her head supported by his arm, and turned away from Mary Kate.

"What are you doing?" she yelled. "Mother!"

Dan could hear his mother's slow footsteps on the treads of the stairway. He rocked Krista gently.

Mary Kate was at his side, her hands on Dan's arms. "Let me have her!" she demanded. "You don't know anything about babies!"

But Dan turned away from her again, and clung tightly to the baby.

"Dan?" asked his mother from the doorway.

"You said I could hold her today."

"Yes, I did," said his mother. "But a baby's a very fragile thing, dear. There are some things you have to be careful about, things you might not think of."

"That's what I told him," snapped Mary Kate. "He's too young! He doesn't know what he's doing!"

"We can teach him, dear," said Mrs. Knox then, walking over to where Dan held Krista tightly in his arms.

Dan looked defensively at his mother. But she smiled warmly at him, and held out her own arms.

Dan offered her the child.

"We can talk about all this tonight at dinner," said his

mother. "There are a few pointers we can all share, don't you think?"

Dan nodded dumbly.

He turned then, and without looking back, left the room.

"Babies have holes in their heads."

"Well, so do you," Dan replied. "Five of them!"

Brian nodded, but dismissed Dan's count. "It's true, Dan. Right at the very top."

"But there's skin and hair there," Dan objected.

"Under that," Brian told him. "If you feel around very carefully, you can almost push in the top of their heads."

"I don't believe you."

"O.K. Don't."

Dan beat Mary Kate to his parents' bedroom a second time. Once more he slammed the door, this time waking a sleeping Krista. She didn't cry out, but her eyes opened at the noise.

He didn't have to climb the crib, and he had only seconds before Mary Kate would be behind him.

He slipped a hand through the wooden bars. He put his hand gently at the top of Krista's skull and patted it. He couldn't really tell anything that way.

He bunched up his knuckles and tapped her lightly on the top of her head. Krista just lay there, content, unafraid.

"What are you doing!" screamed Mary Kate from the doorway. "Mother!!!"

20

Dan was peeling potatoes, an entire bag of them. He stood above an empty wastebasket that was lined with plastic and deftly did what he had been taught to do long ago.

His father worked with him . . . washing the turkey, stuffing it, basting it. Mary Kate would come in later to do the vegetables, mostly frozen ones: tiny white onions in cream sauce, squash, green beans. Mrs. Knox had been excused from Thanksgiving duty, having so recently done her part in giving the family a new life. She was also tired.

"We've sure had a busy time, haven't we, Scout?"

"You mean with the baby?"

"Exactly. Now that you and Mary Kate and your mother have had a chance to talk about taking care of such a tiny thing, is there anything you're unclear about?"

Dan shook his head. What he had learned was that there wasn't a lot he could do for or with Krista until she grew up a bit. His mother and Mary Kate had made it pretty clear that mostly what needed to be done for Krista was changing and bathing and feeding. There wasn't a real list of things Dan himself could do yet, although he had thought of some things on his own. He just wasn't quite ready to do them, and not quite sure how to go about doing them. He did know he would need help. When school started again, he would ask for it.

"At Christmas, Dan, we'll have a fuller house. The reason your grandparents aren't here now is because Krista is so new and tiny. She'll be a lot more fun in five or six weeks. And your mother will be cheerier, too, and more comfortable entertaining."

"Who are my grandparents?" asked Dan, swiping the short blade he used on the side of his jeans.

"Well," said his father, "the Knoxes, my mom and dad. They live in Colorado, which is quite a way from here. And then your mother's family, the Billings, will be driving up from Memphis."

"Are they nice?" asked Dan.

Mr. Knox smiled. "They're all more than that, son. You'll like them, and they'll be crazy about you."

Dan reached into the bag for another potato. "I never had *any* grandparents before."

"Well, of course you did, Dan. You just don't remember them, or maybe you never got a chance to meet them. Not that you'd remember. But I'm sure they were all fond of you, and probably missed you when you went away."

Dan shrugged, and doubted. He didn't know whether he "went away" or had been sent away. He didn't know whether his mother was alive or dead. He knew nothing about his father. But if his mother had given him away, his grandparents—whoever they were—would probably have done the same thing.

Mr. Knox put down the ladle he was using to stuff the turkey.

"The important thing to remember, Scout, is that now you *do* have grandparents, who are going to love you and want to spoil you. And if you take my advice, you'll let them do both."

"Does Mary Kate get spoiled, too?"

"Terribly," said his father. "After each visit by one set of grandparents or the other, your mother and I have to help Mary Kate do a reality check."

"She seems pretty real to me," Dan said, almost under his breath.

Mr. Knox took the knife from Dan's small hands and turned him around. "I know Mary Kate hasn't been very nice to you, since Krista arrived. It's a very complicated thing, Dan. Mary Kate was used to being our only child, you see. Even the times we helped other foster children, Mary Kate was still Queen of the May. But all that stopped when we adopted you. Mary Kate was no less important, but suddenly she had to understand there was another person in the house who was just as important to us—you."

Dan looked down at his shoes, but a thin smile of triumph crossed his lips.

"Mary Kate is mad at us, Dan, at your mother and me. And then she's probably mad at herself for being angry. If we work this through, all the way down the line, she's angry at you, too—not for anything you've ever done, but just for being here, for allowing us to love you."

"She wanted me to go away," Dan said quietly.

"She said that?" asked his father, surprised.

Dan nodded.

Mr. Knox wiped his hands on some paper towels as he thought a second. "Well, good for you, Scout. For not telling us, which would have made Mary Kate even angrier, and for not paying any attention to her. Two very good decisions."

"Will she ever change her mind," Dan wondered aloud, "about me?"

"I'm sure she will. It's hard, Dan, being the star of a show and then suddenly being part of the chorus."

Dan nodded.

"But cheer up, Dan. Between Christmas and New Year's, we'll go up north to close the cabin. Just us guys. Maybe we'll bring along a grandfather or two. We'll leave the ladies here to oooh and aaah over Krista. I only hope the weather holds till then."

"I can carry wood for the fireplace," Dan offered.

"I know you can, son. We'll have heat while we're there, but a good roaring fire is always welcome."

Dan had a thought that surfaced from far away—long-ago, cloudy memories. "Do I have any aunts or uncles? Or cousins?"

His father smiled. "A whole passel of them, all ages. Come spring, I imagine we'll hit the road and meet a few." Mr. Knox frowned just slightly. "What made you think of that?"

Dan shrugged. "I don't know," he replied, and he was being truthful.

21

Dan was happy when school opened again on Monday. And relieved. The long weekend had been wonderful in a lot of ways, but also tense. Mary Kate seemed so distant from everything the rest of the family did. Even from Krista, which surprised Dan. Mary Kate had had to be asked to help her mother with the baby. Dan wanted ever so much to volunteer in Mary Kate's place, but he held back. There was something on Mary Kate's mind that she wasn't going to share with anyone, and sensing this made Dan nervous. Almost afraid.

At the end of the day Dan walked to Ms. Breeze's desk and spoke in a tone barely above a whisper. He was worried that Mary Kate would come barging in as she usually did.

"You did some good work today, Dan," said Ms. Breeze as she looked up at him.

Dan smiled, pleased. "I have to," he answered. "And I need some help."

"Help to do what?" asked his teacher.

"It has to do with a baby."

"I heard about your new arrival, Dan," Ms. Breeze said. "Congratulations."

"I didn't do anything."

"No, but it's nice to have a new baby sister or brother around."

"That's what I need help doing," Dan said quietly. "You see, I'm not a very good reader."

Ms. Breeze waited encouragingly.

"But I have to learn to get better," Dan said urgently. "For Krista. There are a lot of things I need to be able to tell her, to help her with."

Ms. Breeze smiled broadly. "That's a wonderful idea, Dan," she said. "Not many young men would ever have thought about that."

Dan reddened just a bit. "There isn't much I can do now, with the baby, I mean. And it's probably just as well, because I don't know anything yet that's really important. But I need help finding out things."

"What things in particular?" asked his teacher. "Do you have special things you want to share with her?"

Dan thought a minute. "Yes," he said then, "I do."

"Anything you want to tell me about just this very minute?"

"No, ma'am," said Dan. "Just that I need help with my reading."

"Well, Dan, I'll do the best I can, I promise. You can rely on me."

"Hey!" Mary Kate stood leaning against the doorway of the room. "Come on!"

Dan didn't turn around. He stood a moment more, looking straight into Ms. Breeze's eyes.

She winked at him, just ever so quickly, which made Dan feel ten feet tall. "See you tomorrow, Dan," Ms. Breeze said. "We'll start then."

Dan nodded. "Thanks," he whispered, and then turned to walk toward Mary Kate and the doorway and Mrs. Farrow outside.

Ms. Breeze watched her student leave the room. Then she stood up from her desk chair and walked to a window, grinning broadly, looking the way Dan felt.

"What are you doing?" asked Brian Baldwin the next day. "How come you weren't outside at recess?"

"I had some stuff to do," Dan answered.

"What stuff?"

"Stuff for Ms. Breeze."

"Geez, what did you do?" asked Brian.

"Nothing," said Dan. "She just wanted to give me some stuff."

"What stuff?" Brian sounded a little exasperated.

"Stuff," Dan replied simply. He wasn't going to share this with anyone. The books were already hidden below his chair, stuffed into his backpack.

"Extra-credit stuff," Brian announced then.

"Maybe."

Brian waited for more. Getting nothing, he started to turn away and walk to his own desk. "Wimp," he said.

Dan grinned, and let Brian think what he wanted to. He didn't care. He was going to work so hard!

But his confidence and excitement dwindled when he heard the last bell of the day. Mary Kate was standing outside his room, waiting for him.

He collected his things and said good-bye to his teacher.

"You know, this really doesn't thrill me, waiting around for you every day," said Mary Kate as she strode ahead of him down a hallway.

Dan couldn't think what to say.

And he was silent, too, when he saw his mother's van at the curb, with her behind the wheel. Mary Kate bounced into the front passenger seat and slammed her door. Dan got into the back.

"Where's Mrs. Farrow?" Mary Kate asked. "Are you strong enough to be out driving?"

Mrs. Knox nodded silently and glanced once quickly at her daughter. Her face was serious, and angry.

Both Mary Kate and Dan sank into worried silence.

As Mrs. Knox rounded a corner onto their own street, she looked in her rearview mirror. "Dan," she said quietly, "I want you to wait in the car for me."

Dan nodded somberly.

Then he and Mary Kate saw the same thing: a gray sedan parked in front of their house, with the words, stenciled in black on its doors, Child Protective Services.

Dan didn't have to try to read the lettering. The image had been carved into his memory too many times.

Mary Kate shrank into her seat.

Dan shut his eyes and felt cold all over.

After a second he opened his eyes to look again. And then he began to get angry inside.

He had been fooled! People, the whole family, had lied to him!

All the images of life before the Knoxes that he had buried without even knowing he was doing so rose again in his mind.

He wanted to hit someone.

He would, when he got back to the capital.

Boy, would he ever!

22

Mrs. Knox and Mary Kate opened their doors at the same time. Mary Kate stood a moment, looking at the visitor's car, and then she straightened her shoulders, stuck out her chin, and started toward the front door.

Mrs. Knox came around to Dan's door and pulled it open. She reached into the car for one of Dan's hands, which she held firmly as she drew him onto the driveway. She closed the back door of the van and then faced him. "Dan," she said seriously but with a hint of an encouraging smile on her lips, too, "we love you."

Dan looked into her eyes and said nothing. Neither did he nod. He was being betrayed.

Obediently, though, he accompanied Mother, hand in hand, toward the front door of the house.

In the living room sat a nice-looking woman, perhaps thirty, wearing a pale gray suit and sipping coffee. A few feet away from her, at the mantel of the fireplace, was Mr. Knox.

Dan was surprised. He hadn't known Father to come home during the day from work. The garage doors had been closed. He hadn't seen the car within.

Mary Kate was not in the room.

Mrs. Knox pulled Dan into the living room with her, and, sitting in a wing chair, she hoisted him onto her lap. Her arms were around Dan's waist.

Dan would have liked to feel comforted and safe. But he was trembling.

Mr. Knox pushed away from the mantel. "Dan, this is Ms. Moore, from Child Protective Services."

He passed Dan, tousling the top of his head as he walked. In the hallway, he stopped. "Mary Kate!" he called sharply. "Your presence is requested down here."

Mr. Knox turned back into the room then and smiled a thin, tense smile. Ms. Moore offered an equally nervous smile in response.

The four waited.

Mary Kate stood at the threshold of the room. "What do you want?" she asked, looking at no one in particular.

"Come in," said her father.

Mary Kate edged into the room and sat in the first straight-backed chair she came to. She folded her legs and crossed them at the ankles, her hands in her lap but with her fingers laced together tightly.

"Ms. Moore," said Mr. Knox, "perhaps you could bring the children into the picture."

Ms. Moore smiled and set down her cup and saucer. She bent to lift a leather-covered briefcase onto her lap. She opened it and after a second pulled out a piece of paper. "We received this letter in our offices a few days ago," she explained slowly. "It seems to indicate that your family is not quite as happy with Dan as it had hoped."

Dan shuddered. Mrs. Knox held him more closely.

"The letter is signed by Mrs. Knox," said Ms. Moore then. "Or it appears that it was."

Mary Kate looked straight across the room at a window. She did not move.

"In effect, what the letter says is that with the arrival of a new baby, the responsibilities of the family are too great to continue having Dan remain here."

The room was totally quiet. Dan wondered suddenly whether Krista was somewhere upstairs with Mrs. Farrow. He wondered whether Mrs. Farrow could hear what was being said.

"I've come here to find out if what the letter says is accurate, to determine what it is your family wants really to do."

"I did not write that letter," said Mrs. Knox in a clear, strong voice.

"Nor have my wife or I ever considered writing such a letter," added Dan's father.

"Mary Kate?" said Mrs. Knox.

"What?"

"You wrote the letter."

"I've never even seen it."

"Oh?" Mr. Knox walked over to stand beside his daughter. "Then who do you guess might have? Can you guess who wrote the letter?"

Mary Kate shook her head.

"Mary Kate!" her father's voice suddenly boomed.

"What?" Mary Kate shouted back.

"Why did you do this?" demanded Mr. Knox.

Mary Kate stood up, not facing her father, not facing anyone directly.

"He doesn't belong here!" she announced. "We don't know anything about him, or his family, or where he came from, or whether he even wanted to come here! He's in the way! He's dangerous to Krista!"

"I'm not," said Dan in a small voice.

"Of course you're not," echoed Mother.

"Ms. Moore," Mr. Knox said after a moment, "we

appear to have a less than truthful daughter. We're sorry you drove all the way out here to see this."

Mary Kate blushed furiously and spun, running toward the stairs.

"Mary Kate!" shouted her father. "You stand right where you are! You need to hear this!"

Mary Kate froze at the bottom of the steps.

Mr. Knox took a few paces until he was standing between the living room and the hallway. "Mary Kate," he began, speaking back toward Ms. Moore, "is a bright and loving child, Ms. Moore." He smiled despite his words. "In fact, she's one of our three favorite children. But clearly Mary Kate is not as happy as she once was. Her reasoning is her own. I'm sorry that it forced you to make this trip. I'm more sorry that Dan's confidence in us might be damaged, even a little.

"My wife and I love Dan, just as we do Mary Kate and the baby. There is nothing I can imagine that would cause us to abandon him, or to give him up, ever."

After a moment, Ms. Moore smiled and nodded, and began to put back in her briefcase the letter she had brought with her.

In the living room, everyone heard the sounds of Mary Kate's speedy and tearful retreat to her room.

Dan was not included in the family conference that was going to take place upstairs after Ms. Moore left the house. Instead, Father carried him into the kitchen, where he was given a big hug by his mother, and then Mrs. Farrow appeared.

"I bet young Dan needs a treat," said Mrs. Farrow cheerfully.

"What would you like, dear?" asked his mother.

Dan didn't speak. He wasn't hungry. He sat on one of the kitchen chairs motionlessly.

"Don't worry about dinner," said Mrs. Farrow encouragingly. "You won't spoil your appetite."

Dan looked up into Mrs. Farrow's smiling face. "Did you hear what they said?" he asked quietly.

Mrs. Farrow reached out to pat Dan's shoulder. "I didn't need to, honey," she explained. "Your parents feel just the same way I do. We all love you."

Dan nodded, and tears began to fill his eyes. He stopped them. He was too big now for crying.

"So, Dan dear, what can Mrs. Farrow get for you?" asked his mother.

Dan shrugged. Then he smiled crookedly. "Surprise me," he said.

"Fine!" agreed Mrs. Farrow. "You sit right there and close your eyes."

Mrs. Knox bent over Dan. "Darling, we do love you. You're safe. This your home and we are your family. Even Mary Kate."

At the mention of Mary Kate, Dan stiffened. But his

mother's hand was on his shoulder, massaging it. After a few seconds he relaxed . . . slightly.

"We'll just be upstairs, dear," said Mother then. "Close your eyes. Mrs. Farrow will do something wonderful, I know."

Dan closed his eyes. He allowed his shoulders to loosen and he sat back. He couldn't imagine what Mrs. Farrow might come up with. It didn't matter. Not really. He would be pleased by anything she put before him.

It was nearly dark, but a few birds still sang outside as Dan circled the house. He smiled at their calls, thinking that soon, with winter, they would be going south, but he would still be where he was, waiting for them to return in the spring.

He glanced at the stockade fence between the Knox property and Brian Baldwin's.

Suddenly he felt sorry for the other foster children who had stayed at the Knox house. Clearly Brian's mother thought they, and he, too, were different than normal children. Maybe even dangerous. Mary Kate had used that word.

He didn't feel any different, or threatening. He agreed with his mother. Mrs. Baldwin had some strange ideas that weren't very happy ones.

He didn't hear the front door being opened and closed. And he didn't hear footsteps on the faded grass behind him. His thoughts had already flown up north to the cabin, and to his New Year's visit there with his father and *two* grandfathers! For a boy without family, suddenly he was surrounded by them. The sensation was almost real enough for Dan to imagine wrapping himself in this material and snuggling into it.

"I'm not here because I want to be," said Mary Kate from the shadows.

Dan turned around.

"They made me," Mary Kate said unpleasantly.

"They made you do what?"

"Come out to say I'm sorry. But I'm not."

Dan knew this. He decided not to say anything back.

"Maybe you could pretend," Mary Kate suggested, moving a few feet closer.

"Pretend what?"

"That I'd apologized," answered Mary Kate.

Dan shrugged. "I suppose I could."

"Good," Mary Kate pronounced. She turned away for a minute to start back indoors, but she stopped suddenly. "That's not to say," she added, "that I may not change my mind later."

Dan nodded. "O.K."

Dan thought he saw just the slightest trace of a smile on Mary Kate's face, but she had turned again quickly to get inside to warmth, and he wasn't sure.

He stood a moment, thinking. He didn't mind pretending. It was easy to do. It made Mary Kate happier. And it didn't, really, down deep, make much difference to him at all.

What mattered was that he was where he was supposed to be, and that he was going to stay.